HELL:
CITY OF THE KILLING DEAD

Un Libro De Judith Sonnet

A.K.A.

Hell 2
Hell 2: Kingdom of the Flesh Eaters
Demons of the Damned
Cannibal Vortex
Hell of the Unholy Dead IV
My Blade Sings a Violent Song and It Sounds Like Your Name
Entombed City
Curse of the Apocalypse

ISBN: 979-8-89372-635-0

3/20/2024

Imprint: Independently Published

Printed in the USA

Paperback cover and wrap designed by Don Noble

Edited by Danielle Yeager, Hack & Slash Editing

Formatted by Cat Voleur

Praise for Judith Sonnet

PSYCH WARD BLUES

"PSYCH WARD BLUES by Judith Sonnet will take you by surprise. The violence is extreme, the action intense, and the emotions raw and honest. Apocalyptic horror with heart. What more could you possibly ask for?" Gord Rollo, author of *Jigsaw Man*

"Judith once again succeeds in combining gore and emotion. There's not a bad story in this book." Aiden Messer, author of *Pet*

JUDITH SONNET

SUMMER NEVER ENDS

"Wow. This book was something else . . . This one has the potential to be a career defining book for the author." John Lynch, author of *The Warrior Retreat*

"As someone who was forced to go to church camp (aka the weekend from hell), this reading experience was CATHARTIC." Mique Watson, author of *Them*

"A dark and brutal novella with themes of religious hypocrisy and the lengths a parent might go through to protect their children, which in the case of this book is way, way too far." Duncan Ralston, author of *Woom*

HELL: CITY OF THE KILLING DEAD

THE CLOWN HUNT

"Love it. The opening scene is suspenseful and brutal, followed by a strong focus on the main character, Willow. Then the very fast-paced hunt begins. From this point on, if you're looking for carnage, every chapter is practically written in blood. I know one of the deaths will stick with me for a looong time. ("Wishbone!") I really appreciate that it did so much to change up the formula while still feeling like a slasher." Jon Athan, author of *Shared by Two*

"The author warned us that the book would be filled with extreme blood, gore, and torture. She most certainly delivered." A.M. Molloy, author of *South*

REPUGNANT

"This book blew me away. Well written characters, an interesting plot, and extremely gory descriptive kills!" Donna Latham, author of *Finding Heaven*

"Halloween Kills meets The Resurrectionist." Mique Watson, author of *Them.*

HELL

"So, what we have here is a goddamn Italian masterpiece. You like Fulci? You do? Cool. Then you found the right book. This is a great piece that gives you all the Fulci vibes and retains that Sonnet style." Brian Berry, author of *Snow Shark*

"If you enjoy extreme horror, transgressive fiction, or Italian splatter films, you're gonna have an infernal blast with HELL." Brian Bowyer, author of *Flesh Rehearsal*

"If you're a '70's Italian Horror fan, this book is a MUST READ." Michael Louis Dixon, author of *Sick*

"When it comes to horror, Judith Sonnet fucking gets it. HELL reads like a doctoral dissertation on surreal splatter. But a lot more playful, illogical, and icky. This is one novel this year you don't want to miss." Lucas Mangum, author of *Saint Sadist*

NO ONE RIDES FOR FREE

"Just know this book isn't for you if you aren't in the right headspace or can't handle even mild gory horror. But if you want some extreme horror done by a master, this book doesn't disappoint." A.M. Molloy, author of *South*

"Great story, totally icky, but has the power of good storytelling. This is extreme, so be prepared, but Judith does a great job of maintaining the dread throughout." Chris Miller, author of *Dust*

FOR THE SAKE OF

"Something like this is not that impossible in the real world. Every day a new atrocity dwarves the last one." Otis Bateman, author of *Maggot Girl*

"And I thought Edward Lee was grotesque. This book takes it to another level in a good way. Highly entertaining and not for the weak!" Keith Bruton, author of *The Lemon Man*

HELL: CITY OF THE KILLING DEAD

BEAST OF BURDEN

"Interesting characters and prose that pulls you in leads to a climax of super-splatter that will have fans of Extreme Horror quivering in gooey excitation! Not for the squeamish!" William Schoell, author of *Saurian*

"This is Judith Sonnet's Stand By Me, and in turn, she wrote Stand By Me for the metal kids. As a metal kid myself, I appreciate it." Lucas Mangum, author of *Saint Sadist*

Contents

Dedicated, once more, to Lucas Mangum. Who understands these movies even better than I do.

Lots of love, buddy.

Introduction

This book is inspired by my love and adoration of Italian horror cinema from the '70s and '80s. It is intended to read like one of those films, meaning that the dreamlike logic of the story and the bizarre dialogue is intentional. It is written as if it was *dubbed* in English.

If a scene started to make sense, I'd delete it and try again.

Please note that this book is best enjoyed with loud music, popcorn, and an open mind.

It is a crazy read, and it should only be read by the insane!

(Also, if you don't like splatterpunk, you won't like this book. Read at your own risk. I'm not going to spoil the story by giving you specific trigger warnings. If you need a trigger warning . . . you probably won't enjoy this book anyway.)

YOU DO NOT NEED TO READ THE FIRST BOOK, *HELL,* TO READ THIS ONE. THIS IS A STANDALONE WORK, APART FROM ONE OR TWO QUICK REFERENCES.

BOOK ONE

Demon! Demon!

As the world ends, a new one will be birthed. One ruled by the Inninian. A paradise of hedonism and sadism. Governed by the Queen and King, and all shall bask in their Unholy Glory, weeping and perishing!

—*The Text of the Inninian*, author unknown

Dreams of Hell Hopes for Heaven

Lori Lyric awoke with a start. Her nightmare had crumbled around her into pitch darkness, and then she'd been expulsed from dreamland and planted back into reality.

For whatever that was worth.

Lori blinked, rubbed the sleep from her eyes, then yawned like a limber cat, stretching her arms over her head and relieving the tension in her muscles.

Sleep was hard to come by, hard to keep, and hard to enjoy. Especially with all the work she had to do.

"You nap?" Brion Bowyer asked from his desk.

"A little." Lori struggled to stand. She adjusted her skirt and checked her buttons. "What's happened?"

"Not much. No one really knows what the fuck is going on. It's like the apocalypse out there. We've got folks on the scene, of course."

"On the scene?"

"Yeah. There was another shooting."

"I thought you said not much had happened?" Lori bolted toward the desk and looked into the row of screens showing the multiple camera angles that surrounded the anchor.

Bowyer shrugged and tapped his cigarette out in the ashtray. There was a swampy pile of crinkly ashes heaped up in the ceramic bowl that his child had made him for Father's Day. The ashtray was a staple in the control room, but no one used it except Bowyer. Two years ago, his son had wandered into traffic and was hit by a car. After this tragedy, Bowyer struggled to keep his life in order. He countered the trauma and depression by burying himself in his work. In *this* work.

Lori understood. She had her own reasons for staying behind the camera. It was the only place where she was accepted without question. Lori was trans, and it was hard being a modern woman in the seventies when so many people chose to be ignorant and hateful.

"What'd you dream about?" Bowyer asked.

"Huh?"

"You were dreaming pretty loud."

"Oh, sorry." Lori sat in the chair beside Bowyer. Everyone around them was chattering and dashing about, as if they expected the building to collapse if they didn't keep it standing. "I dreamed about a town in Missouri."

"Missouri? You ever been there?"

"No. But I dreamed I was called there . . . and all sorts of crazy things happened."

"Like what?"

"Like . . . demons attacking people."

"It's the stress. It has been a crazy couple of weeks."

"Yeah. Anyone know who's behind all these attacks?"

"Lots of theories," Bowyer sneered. "Some people say something's contaminated the water, but I've been drinking from the tap, and I don't feel like going into a shopping mall and chopping up random folks with a butcher's knife. Do you?"

"Nope. Just bad dreams."

"Maybe that's how it starts. You could be infected already." Bowyer made the sign of the cross.

"Hardy-har."

Lori was tall, curvy, and brown-haired. She spoke in a husky tone and her eyes were blue with weariness. Bowyer was skinny, bald, and deep-voiced. He always had a smile for his friends, but everyone outside of that group thought he was a sardonic stoic. You just had to wait for him to open up to you.

"You wanna smoke?" Bowyer asked.

"Why the fuck not?" Lori held out two fingers. He slotted the cigarette into her hand, then lit it with the tip of his own. Lori pulled in a deep and relaxing drag. She let the smoke seep between her teeth and toward her eyes. It stung and rendered her vision blurry.

"So," Lori said, "tell me about this new attack. What happened?"

Bowyer frowned. "Happened downtown. A guy wandered into the street and started shooting. Witnesses claim he'd dug out his own guts and wrapped them around his throat. Like an organ scarf."

"Yuck."

"We can't show any of it, obviously. So, we've got a row of witnesses being interviewed. The guy in the newsroom? You gotta see him to believe him. Total weirdo. He's blaming this shit on cults."

"Cults?"

"Yeah. Turn yer ears on."

Lori faced the multiple screens. They showed her an omnipotent view of the anchor desk and of the guest sitting adjacent to it.

The guy was normal-looking. Large, bearded, with shaggy hair and dense eyes. His lips trembled and his hands were knotted together. He seemed nervous to speak but unwilling to move. As if he didn't want to share his story—but needed to.

"What's his name?"

"Sergio Bianchi. Italian guy. He's an academic too. A professor at Arkham University."

"Your alma mater?"

"Yup."

"You ever take his class?"

"Nope. He was after my time. Or his classes weren't popular. The way he talks, I wonder what his students think of him. Maybe they think he's crazy. Maybe they think he's a snore. No clue. Be interesting to be a fly on that wall."

"What's he teach?"

"Get this . . . demonology."

Lori shuddered, recalling her detailed and frightening dreams. She'd never had a nightmare like that before. Not in all her years of living.

There are many gateways and doorways to Hell. Each one has its own devil. Lori recalled hearing in her dream.

She listened to the man speak.

The anchor, Keaton Manners, was scolding him. Keaton was brash, young, blond, and a real pain in the butt. He thought he was some sort of Casanova because he was on American television. He'd often show up to work with eye candy on his arms and nose candy on his upper lip. He'd once even gone on the air with a bead of coke dangling from his nostril like an un-melting snowflake. He was also a heavy drinker and had gotten into several fistfights with staff.

But he was popular with viewers, so no one had the balls to kick his smarmy ass and send him packing.

"Let's get this straight for the good people at home, Professor Bianchi," he spoke the man's title like it was a slur. "You expect the good people of this city to buy what you're selling?"

Bianchi shook his head. His jowls warbled. He wore a suit coat patterned with bright eyeballs and twinkling stars. His pants were short, showing off his hairy legs.

"I do not expect you to believe me, but I expect you to heed me. When what this is becomes more obvious, I want you to be prepared. I do not want to incite a panic when I tell you that the occult is real, and I do not want to offend when I proclaim that its actual workings are *not* what you've been told they are. I've seen the signs in the horrific rash of violence that has overtaken our city. Ju-just last week, when Malcom Falk stormed the hairdresser's shop with a machete, do you know what he painted on the wall? You should, Mr. Manners. You reported it!"

Keaton huffed and looked toward one of the cameras. They were quick to shift focus so that the anchor's steely eyes were transfixed on the audience.

"If you'll remember, last week a man named Malcom Falk did indeed force his way into a hairdresser's with a machete. That much is true. He killed three people, taking their heads off of their bodies—"

"He did more than that."

"Okay. He *molested* some of the women with his weapon. Does that make you *happy*? Huh? Do you get off on—"

"Get outta that," Lori heard someone shout into a microphone, diverting this line of questioning. "Christ, Keat. This isn't a bar!"

Keaton coughed and went back to the audience.

"Malcolm Falk was a disturbed individual. He killed himself before the cops could. His apartment was filled with diaries and occult items. He owned a Ouija board, his windows were crowded with crystals, and he hung his landlord's body in the closet. The man was not well. What he did or didn't write on the wall of that hairdresser's shop was the workings of a demented brain."

"Tell them what it was."

Keaton grumbled, "He wrote out a line of script from an ancient book, often called the *Book of the Dead*. It's one a lot of weirdo wizards and satanists quote all the time—"

"And scholars," Bianchi cut in. "The book is a rare one. It's only known to Magickians."

"Don't you mean magicians?"

"No. I mean Magickians. People who practice the strongest form of the dark arts."

Lori felt her stomach rumble. She hadn't had lunch yet.

"This book is called *The Text of the Inninian.*"

"What is that? Arabic?"

"No. It comes from no known language. The Inninian are believed to be a *family* of gods, but their origins and worshippers are unknown."

"Old religion has no place in Christian society." Keaton mugged.

Good. That'll turn the Conservatives on to our station. Lori smirked.

"This religion is older than old. It is thought to be *prehuman.*"

"What's the supposed to mean? This family of gods was worshipped by dinosaurs?"

Bianchi shook his head. "I cannot speculate on what worshiped the Inninian family. I can only say that the words Malcolm Falk wrote on the wall were in the untranslated language found in their sacred text. No one had translated the Inninian bible. No one can! There's no Rosetta stone to corroborate its language."

"Then what's the point of even discussing it?"

"The crazed man wrote the line *Ephith Eck Phintelli Obsolium Mundun.* Then he took his own life by sitting on the machete and driving it into his bowels—"

"Okay, Bianchi!" Keaton barked. "Let's spare some of the gory details, huh?"

Bianchi apologized, then continued. "What makes it curious is this: he wrote these words that preceded a section of the book that appears to be ritualistic instructions. One of which involves a diagram of a human body being skewered—"

"I thought this book was written before humanity?"

"It was! Which makes its accurate illustration of the human body so peculiar. And it makes Malcolm's knowledge of the text bizarre as well because, Mr. Manners, there are only *three* copies of *The Text of the Inninian* in existence!"

"Oh yeah? Well, maybe he went to a museum and saw—"

"I know who did it."

"You know?"

"But no one believes me when I say it was a student of mine. A student who grew obsessed with the ancient book."

"So, how'd he get his hands on it?"

"I loaned it to him." Bianchi's face broke. He looked close to tears. "He's on the streets now, spreading the word like a missionary."

"What's his name?"

Bianchi didn't seem to hear Manners' question.

"But he couldn't have translated it accurately. No one knows the language of the Inninian. Except the Inninian themselves."

"What are you saying, professor?"

"I'm saying that a member of the Inninian family *commanded* this poor man to sacrifice himself. And that he isn't the only one! Mark Richards, who slew his family and burned the body of his youngest son, did so *according to one of the diagrams.*

Patricia Wilkers boiled her own face and peeled it off, matching one of the illustrations in the book *perfectly.* I'm saying that one of the Romanian is here! Here! HERE in our city!"

"You know what I'm saying, Mr. Bianchi?" Keaton shuffled his papers around. "I'm saying we've humored you and your drivel long enough!"

"The madness will spread. It will only get worse unless countermeasures are taken. Soon, the dead will walk through our streets and—"

"Jim? Security? Let's get this fruitcake off our stage. I'm tired of giving him a platform!"

There was a smattering of applause through the control room. Lori and Bowyer did not join in. Their cigarettes were almost to the filters.

The newsroom was interrupted by footage on the street. A new bubbly female reporter was standing next to a Black man with a bloody shirt and shaking hands—a witness to the shooting. He was already speaking before the reporter could introduce him.

". . . crazy guy came outta nowhere. Started firing into the crowd. Shouting in some foreign language I didn't recognize. I tried to stop the bleeding. I tried." He showed off his hands. "She'd been hit in the gut but . . . I *tried*!"

"Did the police kill the shooter?" Lori asked.

"No." Bowyer shook his head. "After he ran out of bullets, he sat on the street and unraveled the rest of his guts by hand."

"Christ. Maybe that weirdo professor had something to say we should've been taking seriously."

"I doubt it. I mean, do you believe in demons, Lori?"

She shook her head. "Not on your life."

In the Tube

Darkness Swallows

BEING A WHORE WAS a whirlwind. Ulma Thompson remembered when she was in high school, when she'd enjoyed the way her peers and teachers lustfully looked at her developing body. Now, she hated the male gaze, even though it hadn't changed.

She'd moved to the city with high hopes.

Those had been dashed.

Sure as shit.

She hadn't made a splash on the stage. She hadn't attracted the wanting hands of a TV agent. She wasn't on a syndicated sitcom. She wasn't fighting with her schedule to make appearances in A-list films. Hell, even exploitation flicks and the movies that played in the adult cinemas didn't seem interested in her.

She didn't know what it was she was missing. She was a pretty woman. Curly-haired, curvy, and luscious. Her lips were plump, her hips had neat little dips, and her legs were shapely. She looked like Venus, fresh outta the clamshell.

She'd been betting on being a success. But eventually, bills needed paying.

Unemployment was up as well. The city was entering a recession. She couldn't even get a straight gig as a waitress.

So, she'd turned to the oldest and grimiest profession known to man.

She spread her legs for money.

And today, they'd been spread as far as they'd go.

She sat on the subway, her bum and cunt on fire. She'd had three men see if they could fit their hot dogs in her buns. They were brothers, and they'd always proclaimed that ever since they were kids, they all wanted to fuck a bitch at the same time.

It'd been hard work, but she'd earned her keep. She'd told them she'd do it for one hundred bucks per prick, so she had three hundred dollars in her purse now. That'd go a ways.

The train rocked and rolled through the darkness. The lights above her crackled and flickered.

Sitting across from her was a sleepy man with a beard and black sunglasses. She thought he might be blind, but some dudes wore those glasses so women didn't know they were being leered at.

Sighing, she looked around at the other passengers. It was a small crowd.

There was a bag lady sitting at the end of the bumping car. She was talking to herself. She was elderly, decrepit, and her face was veiny. She smacked her lips loudly between curses.

On the opposite end, toward the head of the car, sat a studious young man with spectacles. His hair was blond and disheveled. He wore a suit and tie—nothing too formal, but formal enough to stand out in a crowd. He was reading from a book open on his lap. He turned the pages carefully, as if afraid they'd crumble in his fingers. She realized he was also wearing gloves. Not latex hospital gloves or yellow dishwashing gloves. No. *Black* gloves. Made out of shiny leather. It looked as if he'd dipped his hands in ink.

Across from him sat a Hispanic woman with a parched throat and a hacking cough. She was obviously sick but hadn't been able to take time off work to heal. She was carrying a purse stuffed with tissues which she extracted and blew into periodically.

The young man looked up at the ill woman. He frowned, then turned his body so he was pointed away from her.

His eyes caught Ulma's.

He stared for a moment, then sheepishly returned to his book. His cheeks blushed.

Ulma liked it. Liked modesty and innocence. Liked the embarrassment too. Most of the men she worked for wanted to act like tough guys. Like they were all Dirty Harry.

She liked the fact that this boy had been attracted to her but didn't want her to know it.

Smiling, Ulma stood and walked over to his side. She plopped down next to him and spoke in a sultry tone, "Hey."

The boy startled easily. He gulped, shutting his book and pinning it to his chest. "Sorry?"

"I just said hey. How are you?"

"Oh. Fine. Fine." He scratched at a smooth cheek with his black-gloved hand. "Y-you scared me."

"Ain't nuthin' you need to be scared about. I don't bite." Ulma flashed her teeth.

He smiled, relaxing in her presence.

"I'm sorry if I offended you," he spoke properly, meekly.

"No. No offense taken. Actually, I'm flattered!"

"Really?"

"Really. Say, whatcha readin'?"

"Oh. It's just an old book." He showed her its front. "I actually translated this version of it myself. *The Text of the Inninian.*" He seemed embarrassed to be saying it out loud. "Like I said, it's just an old book."

She saw that it was just a notebook. The title on its cover was handwritten. "You like reading?"

"Y-yes. I go to Arkham University. I'm studying—well, it sounds silly—I'm studying Magick."

"Hey! Like David Copperfield? He's so dreamy."

The boy smirked. It was a cute look. "Something like that."

"I'm Ulma," she said.

He shook her hand. "Tanner Fishman."

"That's your real name?"

"Yes. I know. It's weird."

"I like it!"

"Where are you headed?"

"Home," Ulma said. "Just finished a long shift. You?"

"I went to pick up this book and now I'm headed back to my dorm. What time is it?" He checked his own watch. "Yeesh. It's already eleven!"

"Yeah. Tried getting a taxi at first but traffic is halted," Ulma said. "Cuz of that crazy guy. You heard 'bout that?"

"I saw it on the news. They interviewed one of my professors. He apparently witnessed it all."

"Well, I heard it on the radio. Lord. It's scary how *violent* people are these days, isn't it? You think it was always like that?"

Tanner nodded. "You should read some of these old books. Even in the Bible, people were always nuts. Killing each other. Killing themselves. Death has always made a profit."

"Gee. Guess you're right. But I don't know. The world definitely felt brighter when I was a kid." She grew misty-eyed.

"Hey? You okay?"

"Sure. Sorry. Guess I'm close to spilling my guts, huh?"

Tanner smiled. "I've been told I'm easy to talk to."

"Well, I guess that's it, then. I don't know. Came over just to see what you were doing and now I feel like sharing my life story with you. Ain't that a trick?"

Tanner used his gloved hand to wipe away a tear that left a slimy trail down her cheek. His touch was cold and gritty. Not unpleasant but certainly uncanny.

"I've been scared, too," he said. "Scared of everything going on. The city feels like it's about to explode or something."

"Yeah. That's exactly it. Like we're standing on a big volcano."

"Yes. It's enough to make one consider taking this knife"—he reached into his coat and pulled out a hunting knife that gleamed brightly in the flickering light, like a massive, silver teardrop—"and putting it through that coughing cunt's throat." He indicated the lady sitting across from them.

She took the knife by its ornate pearl handle. It felt light in her hand. "Yes," Ulma said, "that makes sense."

"Will you do that for me?"

"Of course."

She stood and strode across the car.

The woman was honking into a tissue when Ulma stepped in front of her. She looked up with blurry eyes and snorted deeply.

"Sorry," she said with a heavy accent. "Was I bothering you?"

Ulma plunged the blade into the woman's face. It slid into the skull like it was made of butter. The woman's brittle bones crumbled, and her flesh was punched in by the weapon. Blood sizzled from the wound, leaping away from her.

Ulma yanked the knife out, leaving a long scar on the woman's face. Connecting her left eye to her screaming mouth.

She drove the knife in again, this time sliding it into the woman's throat. She heard the muscles inside crinkle against the silver surface of the knife.

Rather than pull it loose, Ulma twisted the handle, widening the fissure. Blood fell in a thick curtain down the woman's heavy breast. She shuddered in place, blasting blood from her mouth and releasing wheezy screeches. She writhed in her seat, bracing herself with her arms. Snot dribbled out of her nose and glazed her scrambling lips.

Ulma removed the knife.

Blood pissed from the hole. A stream of ropy gore was followed by a thick, pink mist.

"Jesus Christ!" the man with the sunglasses shouted. "What the hell are you doing?"

Ulma turned back toward her master.

Smiling, Tanner said, "Kill him too."

Ulma dashed down the car, charging toward the bearded man. Yelping, he got to his feet and attempted to run, but his gait was too slow.

Ulma slammed into his back, knocking him off his feet. The large man collided with the floor and squirmed like a worm in upturned dirt. He cried out, “Please, ma’am! I won’t tell no one!”

Ulma sat down on his rump, squeezing her knees on his hips. She held the knife in both hands and raised it above her head.

She stabbed him in the back. Like a swimmer diving into a pool, the pointed tool dove into his flesh. She could feel the edge of the weapon grind against his knotted spinal cord.

The man’s screams were replaced by an earth-shattering howl.

She tore the knife out, then brought it down again, aiming for the space between his shoulder blades.

His legs kicked. His arms seized. His head rocked back and forth.

“Oh, God! Oh, Mercy! Oh, Heaven!” he prayed.

She rocked the knife out. Now, he had two slots in his back. Blood escaped both exits with hot hissing sounds. Like bacon sizzling in a frying pan.

Ulma was covered in blood. It spat out from her victim and coated her front. She loved its hot touch, steamy odor, and tangy taste.

She turned the knife on herself, using it to slice her blouse open and free her breasts. She slammed the blade into the man's back, just to free her hands so she could scoop up palmfuls of blood and rub them onto her tits.

She moaned and grinded against her whining, dying victim.

"Please. Please! PLEASE!" the man brayed.

It was like choral music to her ears. She sealed her eyes and enjoyed the tingly sensation of her nipples puckering. She luxuriated in the stimulation that buzzed from her clit to her core. She rubbed her pelvis up and down the seat of the man's pants. She even enjoyed feeling the shit streaming out of him, inflating the rear of his jeans with mushy soup and tender logs.

Oh God!

Why am I doing this?

Why am I loving it?

Ulma combated the guilt by focusing on her encroaching orgasm. It struck her like a bolt of lightning. Freezing her in place, hands cupped over gory breasts, mouth dime-sized with shock, eyes inflamed with lust. Her whole body shuddered. She could feel fluids leaking out of her pussy and slickening her already-soaked panties.

Beneath her, the man was still crying for God.

She slid the knife out of him. Another geyser of blood bloomed from the wound.

She pounded it into his head. The skull cracked like a baby turtle's shell against a seagull's beak. Blood fizzed out of the gorge and streaked the floor ahead of him. He lay still, dead the second the knife speared his brain.

She pulled the blade, setting it down on the jouncing floor of the subway. With her fingers, she pulled apart the cleft in his head. Strands of gore clung tight, but they eventually snapped like tight rubber bands.

With a grunt, she pulled his head open and allowed his brain to slosh out. The gray organ had been destroyed by her knife, but it was too succulent to discard.

She used her hands to scoop up the mushy tissue, then carried the jellied brain to her mouth and began to feast. It was like filling her mouth with sex. The sensation of putting her tongue against a flabby piece of meat that had once contained *thoughts, feelings, and opinions* was even better than the orgasm that had just rocked her body into oblivion. She went blind with pleasure. Began to drool around the scraps of meaty matter as she consumed it. And swallowing? Feeling that warm lump of tissue go down her throat?

It was as if God himself had put three fingers in her cunt.

Lord!

"In the name of the Father, the Son, and the Holy Spirit, begone devil!" a rancid voice screeched, yanking Ulma out of her euphoric state. She glared ahead at the homeless lady, who was wielding a crucifix. A trinket she'd been carrying in one of the many paper bags that surrounded her. She was scowling. Furious like an interrupted school teacher. She didn't seem to fear Ulma. Even seemed to believe she held some power over the whore-turned-demoness!

Ulma wanted to laugh, but her anger was all-encompassing.

"I know the possessed when I see it! Begone, foul spirit! Leave behind this humble child of God!"

Ulma picked up the knife and stood. The blade was dripping. Ulma was so blood-soaked she looked totally naked, even though she was still wearing her skirt and panties.

"You creature of the Underworld! Get back! Shun yourself from the light of Heaven an—" the bag lady froze. She looked over Ulma's shoulder.

"Oh," she muttered. "Oh, God."

Ulma turned, seeing Tanner Fishman standing behind her, wearing his black gloves and a steely smile. Where once he'd looked cute and innocent, now he was conniving and reptilian.

Tanner was holding his book open.

He read aloud from it, "*Illithian Umost Mirith Pyoth.*"

These four words, he spoke with gravity. Each word landed on the mind like a hammer against a chisel.

The bag lady dropped her cross and yowled like a fighting cat. She clutched her ears and stumbled back, screaming as if a red-hot poker had been put up her ass.

Ulma watched, curious to see what the Magick words were doing to the homeless Christian.

"Pray now, bitch. See if your God loves you!" Tanner declared.

The bag lady struck the ground with her knees. She writhed and wriggled, clutching her head between her fists. Her eyes bugged from their sockets and her teeth clenched together, severing the tip of her tongue. The pulpy patch of muscle flopped out of her mouth and spattered against the floor, adding to the stains left behind by Ulma's second victim.

The lights of the subway flickered, giving the scene a strobe effect. In between flashes of darkness, Ulma watched as the woman's eyes turned red, then shot out of her skull. Like ping pong balls knocked against a swift paddle. The two white bulbs dangled from their sockets, held to her head by thin strands of nerves.

The bag lady cried even louder, tearing her vocal cords as the pain and panic hit her again.

Her hair seemed to move with a mind of its own. The greasy strands swept over her face, then crowded her mouth. They began to travel down her throat like eels in an undersea cave. They detached from her head in ragged clumps, pulling scraps of her scalp behind them. The skin peeled easily, and the blood flowed heavily.

She tore her hands away from her head, ripping her ears away in the process. Blood hosed from her wounds and saturated her shoulders.

More hair pulled itself free, dragging a huge chunk of meat into her mouth. She could no longer scream. The only sounds she released were guttural, choking donkey cries.

She fell back, splashing in her blood and the blood of the man who'd died ahead of her. Her legs kicked around, and her arms shot up toward the ceiling. Her ears sat in both palms, crushed and tattered by the force of their extraction.

Ulma panted heavily, enjoying the unnatural death.

Tanner set his hands on her shoulders. His touch was pure sex and love all in one. It intoxicated her even further.

"You and I will rule this city."

"We'll burn it to the ground!" Ulma cried. "Burn it all down, Tanner."

"That name was a lie. You may call me by my true name."

When he uttered his real name to her, the last fraction of Ulma Thomspon's sanity shattered.

Hearts on Fire Mouth Alight

Lori and Bowyer went to dinner late. It'd been a long day. Bowyer had taken his own nap, just like Lori. He was happy to report that he'd had no nightmares about demons or the living dead, but he did have a crick in his neck which was slow to heal. On their way to eat, he'd rubbed the back of his neck with a long-fingered hand.

At an all-night diner, Lori ordered a hamburger with double cheese and bacon.

"You're gonna give yourself a heart attack," Bowyer said while sipping his milkshake. It was all he'd wanted.

"What's gonna get me first? The greasy food or the cigarettes?"

"Probably the booze."

"At least I'm not a cokehead like Keaton."

Bowyer shrugged. "Guy's an ass but he's a damn good anchor. Always knows how to keep people watching."

"True. Just wish he'd stop saying stupid shit to me. I think he's got a tranny fetish."

Bowyer sneered. "Wouldn't surprise me. You know he goes to some of those dirty theaters in Mill Creek?"

"Oh. He almost got busted by some cops for tugging it, didn't he?"

"Yup. And I know what movie he was watching. Overheard him griping about it in makeup."

"Yeah? Which one?"

"*She-Male Throat Fuck.*"

"NO!" Lori laughed before taking a big, crunchy bite from her sandwich.

Bowyer chuckled and inhaled the last of his milkshake. "You working tomorrow?"

"No. I've got the day off."

"Lucky bitch."

"That's me."

"What are you going to do with your Saturday?"

"Read a book. Hey, maybe I'll find the one that nutcase was talking about."

"I doubt it!"

"You never know. In fact, I'm going to go to Morty's tomorrow and ask about it!"

Morty's was a rare bookshop that Lori and Bowyer had frequented a few times. Bowyer liked reading real literature, while

Lori enjoyed pulp trash. Thankfully for the two of them, Morty procured both.

"Well, happy hunting. Wish I could join you," Bowyer said. "But . . . I might have a hot date tomorrow after work."

"How much did this one cost?"

"Bitch."

"Fucker."

The two smiled at each other.

"No. Her name is Olga."

"Olga?"

"She's Russian. A ballet student. Met her on my commute and we hit it off."

"I don't talk to anyone on the subway."

"You miss out. Lots of interesting folks ride the rails."

"Like Olga."

"Like Olga." Bowyer looked above Lori and smirked." She's pretty. You'll like her."

"Hey." Lori softened. "I'm happy for you. Hope it works out."

As much as she and Bowyer chided each other, there was no animosity or ill will in their friendship. And knowing all that Bowyer had been through before she'd even met him, Lori was certainly happy to see him wading into the dating pool again.

Has he told Olga yet?

About his son?

None of your business, Lori. He'll tell her when he's ready.

"How about you? Seeing anyone?" Bowyer asked.

"Nah. I'm still waiting for the right guy." Lori frowned. "Most of them can't get over the whole transness of it all. And gay guys want men. Anyone who is interested in me is a weirdo with a trans fetish. Like our friend, Keaton."

Bowyer nodded. "Sorry. Wish it was easier out there for you."

"If I go on one more date with a guy just itching to ask me if I've had surgery down there yet—"

"Ugh," Bowyer groaned.

"So . . . it'll just be book shopping for me tomorrow. No steamy romantic evening dates with ballet students."

"I'm not apologizing."

"Good."

Lori looked around the diner. Their waitress was reading a paperback romance at the bar. No one else was around except for a pair of cops sitting in a corner booth scarfing down meatball subs and drinking Cokes.

When she turned her head, she looked out the rain-glazed window. The street was dirty, but it wasn't crowded. A homeless man hobbled down one of the alleys, holding his raincoat tight with one hand and pushing a shopping cart with the other. The wind blew a half-decayed newspaper down the road. The paper flipped and flopped like a fish trying to hurl itself back into a pond.

Overhead, lightning crackled.

"It's eerie out there," Lori said. "Like anything could happen all at once and we'd never see it coming."

"The whole city feels that way. What with all the craziness spreading around. Feels like the world's about to go up in flames."

"That won't happen."

"It might. Imagine if we wake up tomorrow and the crazies have taken over? Or even worse, demons. Like that nutcase was saying."

Lori trembled at the thought. "I don't believe in demons."

"Neither do I. But disbelief won't stop 'em."

"Stop talking like that."

"Too gloomy?"

"Too similar to that nightmare I had."

"Yeah. You seemed wigged out. I should've woken you up, but it was the first sleep I think you've gotten all week."

"Didn't feel like sleep. I still don't feel rested. Every time I close my eyes, the darkness reminds me of that bad dream."

She looked out the window again.

Lori almost bolted from her seat in shock.

"What?" Bowyer turned and gazed out the window.

"Did you see it?" Lori asked, her voice wavering. "Standing across the street. Looking at us."

"No." Bowyer cupped his hands around his eyes and pressed himself against the window. "Damn this rain. What was it?"

Lori shook her head and muttered to herself, "Guess it wasn't anything. I don't see it now."

"What did it look like?"

"I need sleep. That's it. I'm so tired I'm starting to hallucinate." Lori shook her head and looked at the scraps of her burger.

She didn't feel like eating the rest of it.

Not after seeing a corpse standing across the road, staring at her with piercing, glowing, yellow eyes.

Down in the Deep Below

the Smell We Hate to Know

Schmidt Paller knew something was wrong.

The air was tinted with a tart flavor that he hated to recognize.

The air in the sewers smelled . . . like blood.

Living in the catacombs, corridors, caverns, and pipes below the city, Schmidt was used to foul smells. Feces, urine, rot, disease, and rat corpses were a perfume that clung to him even when he ventured out from the tunnels in search of food.

Blood wasn't all that strange, all things considered.

Once, he'd found a little girl's corpse. It'd been flayed and broken, compacted into a corner like the last grocery shoved into an overstuffed fridge. Her little marbled eyes pleaded with Schmidt for mercy.

"Shit on you," Schmidt had responded, crawling over her body to grab ahold of the rusty rungs that led up to the manhole.

"Shit on you" was a phrase Schmidt spoke often.

He said it to passers-by who wrinkled their noses at his distasteful stench. He said it to cops who gave him a hard time. He said it to priests who wanted to convert him. He said it to the women who wouldn't fuck him and the women who would. He said it to other bums and derelicts. He said it to his underground neighbors. He said it to bloated rat bodies that floated like paper boats next to chunky turds and streams of sludge.

He even said it to God on the few occasions they'd spoken.

Now, he was just saying it to the air. The coagulated, musty, hot, blood-scented air.

Somethin' different 'bout this.

Smells bad.

Shit on you.

Somethin' wrong.

Should go up.

Even though it's rainin'.

Shit on you.

Should get outta these tunnels.

Job. Family. Income. All of that.

Shit on you.

Schmidt pawed at his nose with a greasy hand. He was skinny, pale white, and redheaded. His face was dotted with scars and boils. His left eye was sealed up with infection and his mouth was so chapped it looked like a wound. He wore rags, wrapped like a dung-smeared mummy. He didn't know how long he'd been living in the sewers. He barely remembered who he was before the bad thoughts clotted out the good ones and sent him scurrying into the fecal dungeons.

"Shit on you!" he proclaimed as he walked through the tunnel, following the fetid scent.

Schmidt Paller wasn't sure where he was. Somewhere beneath Mill Creek and the stadium. It was dark and dank no matter where he went. Asses all shit the same, he figured.

Didn't matter whether you were rich or poor, yer shit had to go somewhere. Down a pipe. Into a slippery chamber. Into a stygian river, where people like Schmidt did not live . . . but festered.

He turned a corner and saw flickering candlelight. That was a bad idea, lighting a fire down here. Sometimes the methane got so bad it could knock a fella out.

Gotta snuff it.

Snuff it.

Snuff that candle.

Shit on it.

Snuff—

It was coming from around the next corner, painting the mossy walls orange in spastic spurts. Not bothering to be stealthy, Schmidt waddled through the water and toward the light.

Should be dark down here.

Light don't belong.

No sir.

No light.

Fuck God.

Fuck his light.

Licking his lips, Schmidt came around the corner.

He was confused by what he saw.

A lady.

Naked.

Bloody.

But not dead.

She was sitting cross-legged . . . in the air. Hovering over the filthy water. Not even being dribbled on.

The light seemed to be coming from no specific source. There was no flickering candle. Just a strange, orange glow that surrounded the beautiful woman.

Red-haired, curvy.

Gorgeous.

She wore nothing except for a pair of sunglasses that were so dark Schmidt couldn't tell if she saw him or not.

"Wh-who you?" Schmidt muttered.

She smiled, showing teeth so white they burned.

He felt as if he was dreaming. Usually, he only had nightmares. Once, Schmidt had dreamed he'd been dropped into the pits of Hell, where he was consumed by fire and jabbed with red-hot pitchforks.

"I am Ulma," the woman said.

"Shit on you," he spat.

"Do you believe in god, Schmidt Paller?"

How'd she know his name? Was she some sort of celestial informant? Was she sent from God Himself to punish Schmidt for their last meeting?

He'd beaten God up while walking one night. Found him hiding in a tunnel, weeping and crying at what he'd made.

Schmidt had grabbed God by the hair and slammed his head into the crusty wall. Slammed it over and over until it'd been grated like cheese, baring the bones beneath.

Schmidt hadn't felt bad.

God always grew back.

Perhaps the old deity had tuned into some of his old-fashioned Old Testament anger.

Well . . . shit on that!

"Yeah. I b'leeve," Schmidt cawed.

"Not the God of the Christians. Useless whelp! No. The *true* god!"

How was she floating in the air like that? Schmidt wondered. Had to have been a trick. People were always playing tricks on him. Like that guy who'd promised to buy him a beer if he sucked his dick in the john. Schmidt had done as requested but had only gotten a fist to the mouth for his services. No beer. Not even in Heaven, he figured.

Yeah. It was a trick.

Had to be.

Schmidt growled, "I dunno you."

"I'm Ulma," she repeated. "Goddess of Lust."

"And I'm the God of *Death*." A voice surprised him.

Schmidt spun around just as the blond boy drove a fist into his gut. Rather than punch him—like a regular human—the fist went *through* Schmidt. He could feel the bags inside of him deflate as their surfaces ruptured and expelled their contents. He saw blood fly out of him in a whirling slurry, coating the front of his assailant.

The man drew his arm back, clutching Schmidt's liver and yanking it free. The organ oozed bile, squealing and farting in the man's frightening fist.

Schmidt wheezed and stepped back, holding his tummy as it fell apart. Long loops of intestines slipped between his clawed, gnarly digits and sizzled against the soaked floor.

The blood smell was stronger now.

Schmidt looked toward his killer.

A young guy. Handsomely dressed.

Wearing black leather gloves.

Looked like a real person, if it wasn't for his gore-soaked arm.

"This," the man said, holding Schmidt's liver out for him to observe. "This will be the first of many."

Schmidt crumpled to his knees.

It wouldn't be hard to guess what his final words were before he died.

Sweetly Oh, Sweetly

Alex Kern was stalking his next victim.

Young. Delicate.

Like fruit.

Succulent.

He licked his lips and glared. She didn't even know she was being pursued, he wagered. Although women were paranoid creatures. They sometimes walked with their keys between their fingers, like claws. That's how Alex had lost his right eye.

Never again.

Nowadays, he hit them from a distance. He carried a can of foaming bear spray and shot them with it before they even had a chance to realize they were in danger.

He'd then wrapped their head in a plastic bag and raped them as fast as he could before their screams called unnecessary attention his way.

But Kern was rarely confronted with his crimes. These bitches could scream all they wanted, but no one ever came to help. Especially in the park.

This one was going to be one of the best, he realized. She was all alone, and he could hear her crying. She was probably walking away from a breakup, poor thing. Too distracted by her own feelings to realize that she had no idea what real pain was.

Kern picked up his pace, loving the way his shoes sounded on the cobblestone.

He was a towering mammoth of a man, standing six feet, eight inches. His hair was curly and ink black. His nose had been broken multiple times. It looked like a wooden block on the center of his face.

He wore a mesh tank top and a pair of skintight jeans. He loved the way the outfit displayed his favorite weapon: the pendulous power tool that swung between his legs.

He was a handsome man. Macho. Unlike that sad-sack fatso the police had called the Mill Creek Strangler until his arrest, he didn't *need* to rape anyone to get laid.

But Kern *liked* what he did.

He considered it a lot like hunting.

There was nobility in that, according to him.

And now there was a punishment angle to it as well. A hope that he'd get revenge for the one who got away. The one who plunged her house key into his face and scratched it the fuck up!

How had Kern explained the sudden scars on his face to his coworkers? Easy. He'd been mugged. Some Black guy. Took him around a corner, knifed him good, ran off with his money. Left him to die.

The lie had worked.

No one knew he'd been justifiably retaliated against.

And he wasn't going to let it go easily.

Some of his most potent fantasies involved finding that bitch and tearing her up even worse than usual. Dragging her into a dungeon and using knives to peel the flesh off her breasts. Making her eat her own clit after cutting it out from between her legs. Putting a fire poker up her weeping twat and twirling it 'round and 'round and—

He'd been at half-mast. Now, he was carrying a loaded gun.

Moving hurt.

Not enough to deter him.

He readied the bear spray, popping its top off and setting his grizzled finger against its nozzle.

It was close to midnight. Overhead, the moon shone through the rain clouds like a spotlight. It was storming, but not enough to wash anyone out onto the street. Besides, he thought the wetness of the rain would help matters. It'd offer more lubrication.

Kern imagined holding her against the muddy ground, slipping and sliding against her. Peeling her moist clothes off of her dewy flesh. Imagined raindrops clinging to her nipples, magnifying them. Their breath was soggy and humid, mixing together as he forced her to kiss him . . . as he forced his way in.

He couldn't get too worked up.

Kern didn't want to blow his load early.

She might laugh at him.

Pathetic man. Can't even rape without cumming too soon!

Ha-Ha!

No. Not him.

He'd make it feel like forever.

The woman was beautiful. Long locks of black hair. A shapely body. She was wearing a beige jacket and a black skirt. Easy access. A skirt didn't need to be unbuttoned and pulled down. It could just be rucked up.

He hoped she was wearing frilly, romantic panties. Those were his favorite types to ruin.

Alex Kern smiled to himself as he worked his way toward his victim.

In what many people referred to as the real world, he was a functioning member of society. A mechanic who worked late and knew his way around any model you rolled in front of him. He was gifted with greasy fingers and keen eyes—well, now it was only one. But he worked just as well with a single eyeball as he would've if God had given him twenty.

He went out for beers with his coworkers. He went on dates and was even fucking a woman regularly. Her name was Patsy and she adored him. He sometimes wondered if she'd kill herself if she knew who he really was.

He hoped so.

At work, they often called him "Gentle Giant." Because although he was ripped with muscles and looked like the sort of guy that rode into old western towns to dispense lawless justice . . . everyone was convinced he wouldn't hurt a fly.

When he'd made up the lie about being mugged, his pals had said, "I'd have gone after that shit-skinned bastard and shown him what for!"

Kern had shrugged. "Woulda just led to a fight. I just hope he gets his life turned around before he really hurts someone."

"Yer a pacifist, Alex. Glad we didn't have you in my trench in 'Nam!"

A pacifist.

If they only knew.

Patsy had been set up with him in autumn. Now that it was spring, she was starting to talk about commitment. Marriage was on her mind, he could tell. It was only a sesame seed away from dropping out of her mouth.

He didn't know if he wanted to get married.

It'd be harder to hide his secrets if someone was with him all the time. And what would become of the panties he'd stolen from his victims, which he kept in a shoebox beneath his bed? He loved masturbating into those shredded, bloodstained garments as much as he loved cumming in a tight snatch.

He'd cry if he had to throw those out.

No. Every time Patsy brought it up, he skirted the discussion. He didn't know how long he could keep it up. Although spousal abuse was an interesting prospect, he wasn't sure how he could cover that up. So, he would delay the inevitable for as long as possible.

And he'd stalk pretty young women late in the night.

Stalk them.

Hunt them.

Ruin them.

He surveyed his environment. The trees were rustling in the wind. The ground was oozing with rain. The cobblestones were slick and glittery. The hills and mounds were vacant. Even the homeless had turned invisible, hiding in dryer places.

It was just Kern . . . and the girl.

Humming to himself, he hurried his pace. Getting close, but not *too* close. He didn't want to scare her yet.

He reached behind him and pulled the plastic bag from his rear pocket. It had a hole cut into it for her mouth, so he could bite her lips while he humped her. The bag also kept the bear spray locked against her, searing her eyes and flesh, while keeping it far away from his own face. It was a good trick.

He wondered when the media would come up with a fancy nickname for him.

The City Park Rapist.

It didn't exactly roll off the tongue. But, hey, Kern was no writer.

And he for sure wasn't going to be hiring a publicist any time soon.

Some of the bums called him "Baghead." He hated that shit. Made him think of dumb horror movie villains.

"Hey!" he shouted; his voice edged like a blade. "Sweetheart!"

The woman spun around.

The foaming mace hit her right in her weepy little eyes.

She was even prettier in the front than she'd been from behind. Kern whooped gladly as he closed the distance between himself and the lady. Setting the can on the ground, he pulled the bag open with his teeth and wrapped it around her head, entombing her in agony.

She was easy to haul into the nearest patch of bushes.

In fact, she barely fought.

Storm Clouds Call His Name, Demon!

When Lori stumbled into her apartment building she realized she was so sleep-deprived it had turned her loopy. As she fidgeted with her key by her mailbox, she wondered if she looked drunk.

I deserve a few drinks.

Maybe before I sleep.

I could take a glass of wine into the bath with me.

Or I'll drink a beer in the shower. Like men do.

She almost laughed aloud but managed to keep it internal. She didn't need to frighten her neighbors any more than she already did.

Her mailbox was empty except for a bill, which she chose to ignore. She could deal with it another day.

Snapping the door shut, she turned and started for the stairs. The elevator was still sealed off with yellow tape. The building's super had claimed it'd be fixed in no time, but that had been almost six months ago.

Someone was sitting on the stairs. She was startled for a brief moment until she realized who it was.

"Hey, Chaddy!" Lori smiled.

"Girl, is that you?" The old man looked around dazedly, his milk-white eyes seeing nothing. "I'm sorry, Miss. Jus' had ta get out the rain."

"Don't worry. I won't tell." Lori stepped toward the stairs. "It's wet out there, isn't it?"

"Wetter 'n Hell!" the man spat.

Chadwick Burnstiff was a troubled man. Lori had spoken to him a few times when he camped on the street, a tin cup in front of him and a cardboard sign reading *Help Me I'm Blind God Bless* next to him. Chadwick was in his sixties, but he looked even older with his unruly white hair and crinkly skin.

Lori always tried to give him her spare change, and she'd even bought him a meal a few times. Once, they'd sat at an outdoor diner—you couldn't take Chadwick inside due to his smell—and she had asked him for his life story.

Chadwick had told it while eating a turkey and pesto sandwich with French fries and a sweating Coke. Afterward, he'd said it was about the best damn meal he'd ever had in his life.

Lori wished she could do more for him. He refused to use her bathroom for a shower and a shave. He refused her offer to help him find a steady job. Chadwick told her he wasn't fit to work. Wasn't fit for human company.

"Well, you get along fine with me!" Lori said.

"That's 'cuz yer different," Chadwick said. "Us irregular folk gotta be kind to each other. Gotta be oases in this damned desert."

Chadwick had been born blind. His mother had abandoned him at an orphanage where the nuns beat him, the priests molested him, and the other children tormented him because he was the only child in their ranks with Black skin. Not that young Chadwick had known the difference between Black and white since he'd never seen the colors himself. He'd learned how cruel people could be in those days, and he'd learned that their cruelty was as petty as it was unreasonable.

Chadwick was homeless, and he seemed to be happy to stay that way. So long as he got a good meal every once and a while, and he had a few folks to talk to. Lori was honored to be in that rotation.

"Hey, this rain ain't gonna get any better," Lori said.

"I hear the Midwest in yer voice, girl. You ain't forgetting where you come from, are ya?"

"No. But seriously, the rain's gonna stay bad. Why don't you come up to my place? Rest on my couch for the night."

Chadwick held up an arthritic hand. His fingers looked knotted together. “I ain’t no charity case.”

“Wouldn’t have to be.” Lori laughed. “You could protect all my books for me while I sleep.”

Chadwick smiled. He barely had any teeth left.

“Besides, I’ve got the day off tomorrow. Want to go to Morty’s with me?”

Chadwick’s smile dropped. “They got nudie mags in braille yet?”

The two of them laughed. “C’mon. Let me be nice. It’ll even out my karma.”

“Okay. But only because yer bein’ pushy.”

Chadwick used his cane to stand. He held his arm out and Lori took it. She wrinkled her nose at his odor but didn’t bring it up.

“Be honest with me now, woman. How bad do I smell?”

Lori considered it.

“Like sewer juice and sloppy roadkill?”

“Christ,” Lori responded. “No. Not *that* bad.”

“But bad enough?”

“Well—”

“Good. I like stinkin’. Keeps the predators at bay.”

“How so?” Lori asked.

"It's like a shield. When I smell like this, it tells people who'd otherwise mess with me to back off. Like a whatchacallit . . . a defense mechanism!"

"But you'll shower tonight, right?" Lori asked. "Since you're accepting my charity?"

"Sure. Fine. If you say so."

"Made any friends lately?"

"Some kid stopped by and talked to me earlier today. Didn't like the sound of him at first, but we warmed up."

"Someone from the building?"

"No. Maybe. Don't know where he went off to. He left kinda sudden. I'll tell you what, though, I don't gotta see the news to know it! With how wild things have been this week, each new person I meet, I gotta wonder if they're the one."

"The one?"

"That'll go off on innocent bystanders."

Lori shuddered. "I know what you mean. It's got me jumping at shadows nowadays."

"People are rotten. But that's always been true. This, though, is just an all-new kind of rotten."

"You could say that again."

They reached the fourth floor and walked down the hall. Lori was dismayed to see her neighbor standing outside his door, smoking in the hallway.

The man was no older than twenty-one. At first, seeing his age, Lori had assumed he was a student. But Andres Clutcher was not quite so noble.

"Hey, Lori!" he sneered. "When you gonna star in one of my pictures?"

Lori shouldered her way through her door, almost dragging Chadwick with her. She snapped the door closed and locked it.

"What was that 'bout?" Chadwick asked, removing his coat and folding it neatly.

"He makes dirty movies in his apartment. Landlord doesn't seem to care. Some nights—all night—he'll have girls and guys running in and out, screaming like demons. Can't get much sleep when he's working."

"What's he look like? Sounded like a kid."

"He is. Twentysomething. Tall. Black hair. He's not a good guy, though. I hear him beating on women sometimes. When the cameras are off. I don't like the way he looks at me either. Like I'm a novelty. I try to avoid him as best I can, but he slips notes under my door. *Call me. I'll make you a star.* That kind of bullshit."

"You want me ta whup him for you?" Chadwick put up his gnarled dukes.

The air seemed to return to the room.

"Nah. Thank you, but I'm a big girl. I'll kick his ass myself one of these days."

Thunder echoed from outside. It rattled the windows like a passing train. The dusty books on Lori's shelves all quivered like frightened cats.

"Smells nice in here," Chadwick said. "Like an antique shop. A good one! Not one of those mothball joints."

"Yeah. I own a lot of books," Lori said, looking around her lair. "I try to keep them in good condition too."

"Say! Maybe you could read one of them to me someday!" Chadwick said.

"That could be fun!" Lori responded with a genuine grin. "But I don't have any nudie mags, unfortunately."

"Ah, no one reads the articles in them things anyway!" Chadwick shrugged his shoulders.

Another growl of thunder startled the two.

"It's bad out there," Chadwick remarked.

I'm glad you came inside, Lori thought. *I'd hate to think of you out there in the cold—*

Her hallucination from the diner reappeared. She felt her stomach knot up at the thought of what she'd seen.

A demon.

The living dead.

A vampire.

A horror of some sort. Something beyond my comprehension. Something above my pay grade.

She wondered, once again, if Morty had heard of *The Text of the Inninian.*

The storm seemed to grumble, as if it had heard her thoughts and hated them.

When Chadwick spoke again, it startled Lori out of her dreams and back to reality.

"Mind showing me the way to the bathroom, ma'am?"

"Oh, sure. You got it," Lori responded.

"Don't let that storm scare you," he said, misinterpreting the tremor in her voice. "Ain't nuthin' but bad weather. Comes and goes."

"You're right. I'm just being silly," Lori said, taking his skinny, shaking arm and leading him toward her bath.

And still . . . she thought that the corpse with the yellow eyes . . . had been smiling at her.

A Nice Guy Like Me

When Kern came back to his apartment, he was surprised to see Andres standing in the hall. The pornographer showed Kern his gleaming teeth.

"You'll never believe it. The tranny just took a homeless man into her room!" Andres said.

"So?"

"So? She's laying hobos but she won't show up in my pictures. Something's stinky over there. Hey, maybe she beds 'em and beheads 'em. Know what I mean? Like a praying fuckin' mantis!" Andres crowded the hall, looking up at Kern with heavy eyes. "Say, you wanna do another picture? Huh? It's good money!"

"Thanks." Kern scoffed. "But I'd rather have the real deal."

"Money is the real deal, man. Green is the real deal!" Andres snickered.

Kern shoved past the kid and strode toward his room, which was at the very end of the hall, the last door on the left.

He didn't mind Andres's job. In fact, the noise of whores getting railed for blow money was ambient and calming to Kern. But he'd *hated* starring in one of those dirty pictures. Everything had to be coordinated. He couldn't improvise, because what if he turned the wrong way and the camera couldn't see the money shot? Andres had been a no-good bickering know-it-all too. Like he was the God of Sex and everyone else was his underling.

No.

Kern wasn't into that shit.

He liked the real, raw deal. Just as he'd said.

Besides, Kern was spent.

The little bitch had done the trick.

Thinking back on the act almost gave him another woody. His cock was sore.

Kern reached into his pocket and rubbed the fine, silky texture of the torn panties he'd ripped away from her pelvis. They were skimpy, red, and lacy. Apparently, she'd expected the night to end in lovemaking before she'd been kicked out by her boyfriend.

He'd so enjoyed her cries.

"Hey!" Andres shouted. "Yer girl came by today! Boy, now she's a looker!"

Kern froze. "Patsy?"

"Yeah. Said she wanted to surprise you. She seemed really disappointed that you weren't around."

Kern swiveled his head like a hungry owl. "What'd you tell her?"

"Just that you were out." Andres shrugged his shoulders. "I didn't know where."

Kern frowned.

"Hey, I didn't know." Andres held his hands up defensively. His fingers always looked pruned, like he'd just gotten out of the bath. "If yer seeing other ladies, I didn't even hint it."

"Where'd she go?"

"Said she'd look for you at the bar. Said you go there a lot with friends from work. I assumed that's where you were. Are you seeing another lady?"

Kern shook his head. He was looking suspicious. He needed to play this off.

"Yeah. But don't tell." Kern smiled.

"Hot dog. Well, all right, man. Hey, yer secret is safe with me. You can't lock a good guy down, I always say." Andres gave Kern a cartoonish wink and nudged his elbow into the air beside him.

Kern snickered, humoring the wimp.

"But still, you oughta bring her over. Yer gal. She'd make a fine little starlet!"

Kern frowned. He wasn't going to whore his old lady out for Kern's amusement. Part of the appeal of Patsy—and the reason why he kept her around—was that she was dedicated to his cock. Married to it. He could call her up and she'd come running, despite the heavy rain. And he wasn't interested in sharing what was his. Especially not with a horny pipsqueak like Andres.

"Hey, Andres," Kern scolded.

Andres's smile diminished. He could tell by Kern's tone that he'd stepped out of line.

"How many venereal diseases do you have?" Kern asked.

Andres cocked his head and pocketed his hands. "None, man. You know I keep it clean."

Kern bared his teeth. "Right. Sure."

He flung his door open and snapped it shut behind him, leaving Andres on a sour note. He knew that question would bother the kid all week. Maybe longer.

Heard he has the clap. Heard it feels like he's got a rod of solid wax in his pipe. It's why it always looks hard, no matter what! Bet it hurts to piss.

Kern flipped his light on and stamped into his apartment. It was bare-bones. He had a sofa, a dingy kitchen, and a few houseplants—gifts from Patsy—he'd been neglecting. Several fruit flies whirled mechanically around a naked bulb implanted in the ceiling.

Outside, lightning flickered.

Kern removed his clothes, leaving them in a muddy pile by the door. He bent over and dug the panties out of his pocket.

His bedroom was even sparser than his living area. There was a vanity mirror, a set of drawers for his clothes, and a hamper—another gift from Patsy. He stood nude in front of his mirror, inspecting his chiseled body with his rough fingers. He was hairy, dark, and his breath seemed to ripple his flesh.

He tied the panties in a knot around his prickly shaft. In seconds, he'd hardened.

A Visit to the Bookstore

When Lori awoke, the sun was shining. It was a relief after last night's storm.

She went to the window and cracked it open, inhaling the starchy scent of humidifying rain and city smog. Not a great smell, but it woke her up better than a cup of coffee.

She sealed her window before going to the bathroom to ready herself. Recently, she'd been sitting behind the desk while Manners spoke about an intruder who scaled buildings and scuttled through unlocked windows. It made her paranoid enough to keep hers locked, even though she doubted such freaks were active at seven in the morning.

After washing her face and doing her hair and makeup, she dressed for her excursion. Wearing a loose sweater and jeans, she walked into her living room, where Chadwick was snoozing deeply.

Probably the best night of sleep he's had all year, poor fella. Wish he'd accept more help.

With Chadwick's background and the abuse he'd suffered as a boy, Lori was sure he was skeptical of help. It honored her that he trusted her enough to accept some hospitality, even if it was only in fractions.

He'd bathed and combed his wiry tufts of white hair. He smelled like her shampoo, which was a good change of pace. She wished she had new clothes for him. Maybe she could talk him into letting her wash what he had.

Just when she was considering letting him sleep in, his eyes burst open. They were pale white, like curdled milk, and startled her.

"Lori? That you?" He sat up.

"Yes! It's just me," she affirmed.

Chadwick put a gnarled hand on his chest and panted. "I had 'bout the weirdest dream I ever did have. Lord."

"Weird dreams are catching. I had one, too, just yesterday," Lori said, walking toward her kitchen. "Come on. A little coffee might help."

Chadwick grunted up to his feet, using his cane to steady himself. He hobbled toward the sound of Lori's voice, felt the air until his hand met the chair, and sat down easily. "Lemme ask ya somethin', girly. You believe in spirits?"

"Like ghosts?"

"Ghosts. Demons. Angels. All of that."

"Can't say I do," Lori said.

"Ah. A modern woman."

"Yes. A victim of sensibility and skepticism. Sorry to disappoint." She smiled.

Chadwick nodded. "You live as long as I do, that doubt starts to scuff off. Like the tread on a tire. Eventually, yer bald on a road that never goes the direction you expect. That make sense?"

"I guess. It's funny you should bring it up. The book I'm hoping to find . . . it's on the occult."

She brought a steaming cup of coffee over and guided Chadwick's hand onto its handle. "Be careful. It's really hot. I'd let it sit."

"I got a tough tongue." He took a gulp without wincing.

Together, they left the apartment. She was thankful that the creep across the hall was a late sleeper, and the giant who lived at the end of her floor wasn't there to glower at her and her friend. Chadwick spoke all the way down the stairs and into the street, describing his dream to her at length. In it, he'd been the lead singer of a groovy band, but he was having trouble keeping musicians because they kept dying on him in increasingly bizarre ways.

"One fell down a flight of stairs and landed on the bottom floor. But that wasn't what killed him. It was the pit of barbed wire he had fallen into! He got all tangled up in it and was fighting and clawing his way back toward the stairs when a wire went around his neck and, well . . . "

"Oh God! How terrible! I wouldn't feel rested at all if I had a dream like that."

"What was your dream about?" Chadwick asked as she guided him down the street. They walked at an easy pace, heading in the direction of Morty's. It usually took Lori twenty minutes to get to Morty's from her place, but with Chadwick, she figured it'd be thirty to forty. He walked unsteadily and slowly, testing each footstep before it landed.

"Last night? I didn't dream at all. It was earlier in the day when I was trying to catch a quick nap at work," Lori said. "Couldn't have been sleeping longer than thirty minutes, but it was like I lived several days in some alternate world."

"What was it?"

"It was in the future. Not too far. Just the '80s. I was a published writer, believe it or not!"

"I'd believe it with how many books you keep."

"I like reading them, not writing them!" Lori chuffed. "Anyway, the dream was set in some small town which had been overtaken by a demon. Some other survivors and I had to go underneath the town, into these catacombs, to find the demon and kill it. It was strange. It felt so real, but I don't know how to describe it now that I'm awake."

"Whaddya think it means?"

"I don't know. That's one reason why I want to go to the bookstore today. We had some guy on the show yesterday, and he was talking about old demon gods. Saying that all this recent craziness is being caused by them. It didn't sound like what I'd dreamed . . . but it was close enough to spook me. Oh, watch out." She tugged him over and a biker zipped by, not even bothering to decrease his speed. Lori tsked. "Isn't there a bike lane?"

"What's this book you want?"

"Something called *The Text of the Inninian*. The nutjob on our show said it was super rare, but there's always a chance Morty will have a lead. He knows just about every bookshelf in the city, front to back."

"*The Text of the Inninian*?" Chadwick swallowed a lump.

"Yes. Have you heard of it?"

She was surprised when he nodded. "There's talk. The homeless here, we've got our own system, separate from yours. Our own government and hierarchy. Recently, there's been fighting. Y'all don't see it. It happens in back alleys, in the dark shadows of the park, and in the sewers. I keep out of it. I'm old enough to be respected and weak enough not to be troubled with. Most of the gangs just walk right around me to get where they're goin', and I like it that way. But I hear a lot more than anyone thinks I do." Chadwick rubbed his nose with the heel of his hand. His eyes flicked back and forth beneath their lids.

"I hear all about the violence you've been reporting on. And I hear who it's credited to."

"Someone's been taking credit?" Lori gasped. "How come no one has told the media?"

"Don't think it'd matter. Someone probably has and got laughed away. I'm surprised yer 'nutjob' even made it on the air."

"He was saying that all the violence was matching a series of rituals in this old book—"

"That's what I heard too. That a group has shown up beneath the city. Some folks say it's led by some outsider. A kid, really. They call him 'The Young Prince' in my circles. He claims to be an *Anninian*. I heard that from Whistler, a dude I sometimes play chess with at the park. You've probably seen him. Wears fur even in the summer. Anyway, Whistler was telling me he was rummaging around for food when he heard crying coming from an alley. He wandered toward it, not wanting to stand by while he assumed someone was bein' robbed or molested. And what he saw . . . it'd curl yer toes. Not even sure I should be describing it."

"Please. I'd like to know," Lori said.

"Well, Whistler came around the corner and—it's crazy but this is what Whistler told me—he saw a young woman tied to a crucifix made from thick wood. The cross was leaned up against a brick wall, seeing as there was nowhere ta plant it in the concrete. She was naked and crying. But she wasn't crying out of fear. No. She was smiling so wide, Whistler said her face was about split in half. He ran over and went to untie her, but she snapped at him, saying, 'Don't you dare! I'm a willing sacrifice, old man! Don't you ruin this fer me!' Whistler didn't know what to do. She insisted that he leave her be, but he couldn't just abandon a poor lady who was in pain. Then, someone else joined in. Another homeless, only unlike me and Whistler, this one's got a bad reputation."

Lori listened closely, trying to picture the scene that Chadwick described. She was having trouble with the finer details.

"This guy is named Bark. You ain't seen him. He tends to live underground. Legend says he once stole a baby from a stroller and spit-roasted it. Whether that story is true or not don't matter because Bark acts bad enough to keep it believable. Anyway, Whistler thought he was in deep shit because if you get on Bark's bad side, he'll mess you up. Mess you up so bad you won't walk again. Whistler started apologizing, even though he ain't done nuthin' wrong.

"He said Bark walked right past him and went over to the woman. He pulled one of his big hunting knives out from his coat and speared the lady right in the side. She quivered and cried but didn't scream. Whistler said Bark pulled the knife out and began punchin' it in and out. Until her side was mashed in. Whistler said he never saw nuthin' so disturbing in all his years.

Then, when the woman died, Bark turned around and spoke to Whistler, acknowledging him for the first time since he'd come on the scene.

"You know what he said, Lori? 'This is to the Inninian. May we all suffer and be accepted.' Then Bark, this hard-ass motherfucker, slit his own throat wide open and died on the spot."

"Jesus!" Lori breathed.

"Jesus ain't got nuthin' to do with it. Whatever this Inninian group is, they demand something more than confessions. They are wanting blood, Lori. Blood and misery. I don't know if snooping around them is gonna be a good idea."

He shivered suddenly, as if something had touched him.

"I think I need to know," Lori said. "Especially now. What if there's a way we can stop them? If this truly is all linked to some archaic religion, I'd rather know than keep my head down and walk by when more and more people start dying."

"Yer a good girl, Lori, for thinking that way." He patted her hand. "But some things can't be helped. If they could convince a violent man like Bark to kill himself, they must be pretty persuasive, whoever they are."

"What have you heard of The Young Prince?"

"Not much. He's kind of a messianic figure, from what I gather. Some people say they've seen him perform miracles, but no one wants ta get specific about it. I gave up asking. Decided I didn't need enemies."

Lori nodded. He was right. Chadwick was exposed and vulnerable. He wasn't privileged enough to dig through something dangerous like this, especially if his findings were ignored. She wondered now if it was only his academic status that earned Professor Bianchi his airtime on the news. If this Inninian cult was really doing all this damage, then maybe her supervisors had shrugged off several truthful letters and tips from the city's homeless. Perhaps the police even knew about the Inninian and had laughed it away as the ramblings of schizophrenics and drunks.

Well, if a cult of some sort is at work in my city, I've got to do my part to put a stop to it. However miniscule my part is. And that means asking around about it.

Maybe this Whistler character would be open to an interview.

She doubted it. She was enormously lucky to have Chadwick on her side and to have earned his openness. The rest of the homeless would scatter if she approached them. Even if she promised to take their word seriously, how far would that get her?

"Promise you won't get in any trouble, Lori," Chadwick said. "Promise you'll just leave it be if it gets scary?"

Lori gulped. "Yes. I promise."

"I'd hate ta think of anything bad happening to you."

"I'm a big girl, Chaddy. I can handle myself."

"You say that now . . . but if this shit gets as bad as some folks are telling me . . ." his voice trailed off.

"What are folks saying?" she asked.

"That it's the first signs of doomsday. That the Inninian cult wants to see the end of the world."

Now it was Lori's turn to shiver.

When they came to Morty's, Lori was no longer excited about enjoying a leisurely hour strolling through the shelves. She had a more defined purpose now, and it was laced with unnerving vibes.

The storefront was modest. There was a window piled high with bestsellers—and this was the *only* space Morty had dedicated to popular books. The rest of the shelves were filled with rare gems and treasures. The kind that one never expected to stumble upon when one was casually sifting through books.

Lori spent enough time at Morty's to be recognized by all of the staff. Yet, Morty himself refused to learn any of his regular customers' names. He was a crotchety old man with a bad smoker's cough and a bald head.

When Lori brought Chadwick in, she was happy to spot Miranda Ascone sitting behind the desk. The woman smiled attentively, closing her copy of Ginsberg's *Howl* right as the bell tinkled over the door.

"Lori!" Miranda had long, platinum blonde hair, a hawkish grin, and wore a multicolored shawl. She was a hippie in remission, the joke went.

"Hey, Miranda. This is my friend, Chadwick," Lori introduced.

"Pleasure to meet you." Miranda stood. Her desk was surrounded by books. Morty's was constantly overstocked as their prices scared off anyone but ardent collectors.

"Pleasure's mine." Chadwick smiled meekly. "Smells just like Lori's apartment here. All these old books."

"Yes. Lori's a frequent shopper. If we kept tabs, she'd be in serious trouble," Miranda said with a laugh.

"Hey. I was actually looking for something specific today," Lori said.

"Yeah? What can I help you with?" Miranda walked around the desk and led the way toward the nearest shelf, which was stuffed with vintage science fiction pulp magazines.

"Did you watch the news yesterday and see the interview we ran with that university professor?"

"Sergio Bianchi? Yes. He's another frequent flyer." Miranda scowled. "Not a very nice one, though, if you don't mind my saying. Very uppity and pushy. Morty hates him. Only accepts his money when he has to."

Chadwick limped behind the women, following their chatter. He walked with his cane, being careful not to strike the towers of books so hard that they tumbled.

"Whazzat?" a persnickety voice yodeled from the back room. "We gettin' robbed again?"

Miranda sighed. "It's a customer, Doc!"

"Oh. Well, tell 'em we've got a sale on popular books!"

They *always* had a sale on popular, modern books. Morty couldn't stand them and wanted them out of his store as fast as possible.

"You heard the man," Miranda said.

"I was looking for the book Sergio was talking about. He claimed there were only a few copies in existence, but I don't know if I believe a word he said."

Miranda hesitated. "The one about those ancient gods, right? *The Text of the Ininian*?"

"That's the one."

"Well. He was right. The original text is very rare. But he got it wrong when he said it had never been translated."

"Really?" Lori asked, wide-eyed.

"Yes. Someone made a translation of it last year. He brought us a bunch of copies, but Morty refused to sell them. He says it would be the same as selling fliers to rock shows, whatever that means. He threw them out. Funny thing, though, I went to the trash to dig them out—thinking that young man's work shouldn't go to waste—and they were gone. Every book had been taken out of the garbage."

"Who was the translator?"

"Had a strange name. Not easy to forget. Tanner Fishman." Miranda picked through the occult section and came back with a leather tome. "Here. This is the only book I've found with references to the Inninian, other than Tanner's translations."

"What's it called?" Chadwick asked.

Lori read the title aloud, "*Cults and Their Practices*."

"It's not incredibly informative, but it's the best I can do. Sorry, Lori," Miranda said.

Lori opened the book and found its price. It'd been penciled in on the upper left corner of the first page. Only ten bucks. Considering the steep prices Morty usually offered, this was a bargain.

"I'll take it. Thanks, Miranda."

"Sure. If I ever run into that kid again, I'll tell him you're interested in his translation."

"How'd he translate it anyway? The way I understand it, the old book was written in an unknown language."

"Well, this brings his credibility into suspicion, Lori. But he claims he heard that book spoken to him and transcribed it through . . . his dreams."

Chadwick grumbled, "Sounds like a scam to me."

"It could be. But I talked to the kid. He seemed pretty sound, all things considered. He said he was passionate about getting the book into the public's hands but that his findings and work were being suppressed."

"Sounds like crazy talk to me," Chadwick insisted.

"It could be. But it'd make an interesting read," Miranda said.

Morty hobbled out from the back of the store. His glasses sat askew on his blistered nose. His pudgy eyes looked like brown drops of pudding. He was holding a large book against his scrawny breast.

He glared at Lori, then glared even harsher at Chadwick. Lori was thankful her pal was blind, just so he didn't have to endure such a withering stare.

He can tell Chadwick isn't a paying customer. He can also tell Chadwick isn't like the rest of us. That Chadwick's status makes him "lesser."

It disgusted Lori.

She often received such stares from people.

She was sure Morty would be glaring if he knew that Lori was trans. He seemed to have a very closed mind. She'd heard rumors that Morty used to have a sign that said *No Coloreds*, too, but she'd marked those off as hyperbolic. Now, with the vehemence in his gaze directed at Chadwick, she wasn't too sure.

Sniffing, Morty waddled over to a shelf and slid a book into place. He fussed with it for an unnecessary amount of time, keeping his eyes trained on Chadwick all the while.

Lori walked Chadwick and her book over to the desk. Miranda joined them, quickly taking Lori's cash and making change.

"I'm sorry we couldn't do any more for you," Miranda apologized. "But hopefully this helps."

"I'm sure it will. Thank you, Miranda."

"And it was nice meeting you, Chadwick!" Miranda said.

"Same to you!" Chadwick responded, showing off his rotten teeth and doing a neat bow.

When they left the store, Chadwick asked, "Didn't you want to stay and shop around longer?"

"No. I'm starved," Lori said, securing her arm around his and walking him toward the nearest café.

A Feast for Hungry Cats

"Filthy Black bastard," Morty muttered.

"That's no way to talk!" Miranda scolded.

"I'm sorry, Miss, is *your* name on the storefront? Do you pay the bills here? Thought not," Morty huffed as he waddled over to the standing ladder and began to climb. He knew there was a book by Dickens up there that would sell pretty easily if it was in reach. A first pressing of *David Copperfield*. The ladder jangled precariously. He knew he should have invested in a sliding ladder like they had at the library, but he felt that doing so would be admitting some sort of defeat to a nebulous someone.

"I just can't believe you sometimes, Morty!" Miranda was aghast. "Lori is one of your best customers, and you look at her like she's trash!"

"Trash. *Humph*. Something *is* odd about that girl. I can't put my finger on it, but there's something queer 'bout her. Ah.

Maybe she's a she-fag. You ever considered that? Total modern degeneracy, the faggots. Used to be men were men and girls were girls. Now we've got an entire confused generation—"

He heard the door clang shut.

Miranda Ascone had left.

Morty was disappointed. He stayed at the top of the ladder, looking around to make sure she hadn't just moved into the shelves, and that it wasn't the wind that had blown the door closed. But, alas, his best employee had disappeared. She'd probably scribbled a note out that read *I QUIT* and left it near the cash register. That's what the last girl had done. But that girl had left on an entirely different principle. Whereas Miranda seemed to be driven away by Morty's mouth, the former employee had left due to his hands.

Roman hands and Russian fingers.

Snickering at the memories of her firm buttocks, he wavered on his perch from the ladder's top. "They all leave." He laughed. "Bitches. The world is full of bitches."

He began to scale down the ladder when there came a sudden sound of thunder and lightning. Not from outside, but from above and around him! Morty felt his heart seize and his limbs go limp. The Dickens book tumbled out of his hands and smacked the ground, landing on its cover.

Morty clung to the ladder, scrambling for balance. But it was too late. The precarious ladder wobbled, jumped, then seemed to spin out from under him! Morty cried out as he fell. His noises were cut short when he landed on a bookshelf. Its hard top drove into his spinal cord. He rolled, then slumped down, dragging a stack of books with him.

When the room stopped twirling, Morty lay on the ground, frozen in agony. His legs were askew, and his arms rested helplessly by his side.

He tried to sit up, but he felt only a cold numbness below his raggedy neck.

Whimpering, Morty's eyes darted around in his skull, hoping that Miranda would return to the store, see there was trouble, and call an ambulance.

He croaked like a frog and managed to wriggle in place. At least he wasn't totally immobile, but he wasn't sure he could make the journey from one end of the bookstore to the other, where the phone was. Not with all the stacks and piles he'd accumulated.

Please, Miranda, come back!

I'm sorry for all I said!

Just come back!

Morty wanted to weep. He held his tongue and his tears, praying that, if not Miranda, someone would wander in.

What had caused this? The sound of thunder? Where had it originated from? He was perplexed by the whole event. What he did know for a fact was that it had been the blow to his back that had rendered him motionless.

Will I be paralyzed for life?

God, I'd rather die than live as an invalid!

Morty wanted someone to blame for this. Someone other than himself and God.

Things were going fine until the she-fag and her colored pal wandered in!

They cursed the place!

It was preposterous, even by Morty's standards, but he was happy to cling to hate while fear roared over him like a tsunami. It was, after all, about the only thing Morty had left.

He twisted and turned, but the movements inspired pain and didn't move him any farther from his position.

He heard a sound. Something skittered across the floor. It moved organically and clumsily.

An animal?

He hoped not. He'd kept the store as vermin free as possible. Even with all these old books, he'd made sure that not even a dust mite had come to invade his sanctuary.

So, what is it?

Maybe it's just a few more books falling over.

Lord, I hope they aren't too damaged!

He turned his head and looked glumly at the books piled around him. A few had bent covers.

He heard another noise. More skittering. Little claws scuttling over the wooden floor, prancing.

What the fuck is that?

He lifted his head with a grunt.

He watched as the black cat hopped from the floor onto the desk. It sat proudly, kneading its paws and tilting its head. It released a soft purr, which sounded like the hum of a distant car.

"Shoo! Scat!" Morty barked. "Get out of here!"

The cat remained where it sat, watching him curiously.

Mort heard another noise. This one from beside him. He turned just in time to watch a plump tabby bolt by. Its orange fur reminded him of sorbet. It jogged down to his feet, danced over them, then leapt onto a nearby shelf, where it balanced riskily. Its eyes glinted toward the fallen man, transfixing him.

Two cats?

How did two lousy street cats find their way into MY store?

I should have them skinned and exterminated.

I'll pin their severed tails to my shop door as a warning to their brothers!

I'll even eat their bastard brains out of their nimble little skulls.

Another cat came around the corner, startling Morty. This one was sleek and silvery. It looked skinny and feral. Its mouth hung open and drooled foam.

Oh, no. That one is sick.

If it bites me—

"Help!" Morty wheezed. "Oh, please, God, help!"

A fourth cat raced around him and joined the tabby. Then a fifth leapt onto the desk with the black cat.

Where were they coming from?

Morty's head turned back and forth as he caught sight of even more cats finding their way into his safe haven. Some of them looked like house pets, while others were mangy and disturbed. One had a flat face and missing eyeballs, the result of a vicious fight, which had left searing claw marks all over its skinny body. Another looked as if it had just been groomed with a pearl-handled brush, its silky fur powdery in the sunlight.

There were dozens of them . . . and then a dozen more. Before long, the store was as crowded with random cats as it was overstuffed with books.

"Please!" Morty whined. "Someone! Please!"

A black cat cautiously strolled toward him, its hips shifting visibly beneath its matted, grungy coat. It held out a forelimb, unsheathing its needlelike claws.

"Please!"

The cat raked down the side of Morty's left leg, pierced his pants, and shredded the flesh. Even though he was paralyzed, he could feel the hot pain and the instant swelling. Blood streamed from the trenches, wetting his clothes and pooling beneath his limb.

"No!" Morty brayed. "Oh God!"

The cat began to lap at the streaming blood like it would a dish of cream. An orange one joined it, sucking from the wound directly with its sandpaper tongue.

Another cat walked up to Morty's belly, then stood on his chest. The creature purred loudly, content to hold Morty's gaze.

"Please. I didn't . . . I didn't do nuthin' wrong," Morty began.

The cat swiped at his face. Its claws dredged his right eyeball out of its socket, as if it had picked an olive from a compost pile. There was a blast of wet pain and then a spattering spray of blood, which coated the feline's smiling face.

It drew its paw toward its mouth and began to gnaw on the plump eyeball. Morty watched in horror as his right eye was chewed, spat up, then chewed again. It was a deflated sac of gushy liquids and tense film now. No longer a solid orb, but a flattened baggie.

His good eye roamed, taking in the sight of the encroaching cats. Spurred on by the spilled blood, the beasts were yowling and salivating.

"No! No! Get back! I'll kill you! I'll kill all of you!" Morty cried.

Another cat struck, puncturing his cheek and ripping it open. The flaps of skin hung loose, exposing his back teeth.

He opened his mouth to scream, but a cat stuck its head into his yawning maw and sank its quilter's pin teeth into his tongue. He fought the cat, shaking his head and grappling with its furry dome, but before he even thought to bite down on the critter and crush its skull, the cat was dashing away. A ropey strand of shredded muscle hung from the feline's mouth.

My tongue! Oh God! They took my tongue!

The cats were surrounding him. He inhaled their fur, their musky scents, and their dribbling spittle. They clawed at every exposed part of him, tearing holes through his throat, in his belly, and chewing on his flimsy hands like they were toys. In no time at all, they'd degloved all ten of his fingers, exposing the red meat and the knobby knuckle bones.

He gulped in mouthfuls of blood and stray patches of fur. The cats were becoming coated in his fluids. They rolled around happily in his grimy expulsions.

Morty turned his head and expelled a soupy broth of bile and vomit. Immediately, two cats began to lap at the pool of sick, just content to eat whatever he had to offer.

I'm going to die this way.

No one is coming to help.

I'm going to be eaten until I die—

He heard the door swing open.

Thank God! I've been saved!

He looked up just in time to see Miranda run into the store, swinging a butcher's cleaver over her head.

She's going to chop up these feral animals and I'll be saved! Oh, God! Thank you! Thank you!

The cats scattered, but Miranda seemed not to notice. Her glaring eyes hit her target, and Morty's face fell with disappointment.

Without shouting or yelling, Miranda Ascone drove the cleaver down into Morty's head. He felt and heard his skull crack, and then his good eye was swaddled in running blood. It poured out of him like wine from a busted jug.

She removed the cleaver, then thrust it down once more, this time chopping directly into his face. He heard the gristle in his nose crackle as the organ was scraped away from his face, leaving behind a gushing, red cavity.

Through frayed lips and around a broken tongue, Morty moaned, "Wh-wh-why?"

"This is for The Foul Twins!" Miranda proclaimed, using both hands to hold the cleaver. "You should have believed in them!"

She threw her body into the finishing blow.

This one divided Morty's head into two wilted halves.

And in the Dark there are Shadows

"So, what'd ten dollars get you?" Chadwick asked.

"Not much." Lori sighed, flipping through the pages. "I haven't found any reference at all to the Ininian. I'm sure it's in here—Miranda wouldn't lie—but I'm betting its nothing substantial."

'Well, she warned you."

"That she did. How's breakfast?"

"Splendid." He wiped his mouth. "I ain't eaten like this in ages."

"Well, we should hang out more often. I like having you around."

"I'll consider it, Lori." He smiled.

Lori snapped her book closed and leaned back. They were sitting on the outdoor patio, eating pastries and enjoying the weather.

Not too chilly, not too hot.

"You really wanna know all this crazy stuff, huh?"

"I do."

"I bet that professor will talk. Sergio Bianchi? Sounds like the kind of guy that likes to open his mouth. Hey, maybe you could take one of his classes!"

"I'm past enrolling in college again." Lori laughed.

"Well, I'm sure you could stand ominously in the back." Chadwick twiddled his fingers.

"Will you go with me?"

"Can't. Not today. I'm actually meeting Whistler for a game of chess. The bastard may be cheating me, seeing as I can't see the board, but it's good exercise!"

Lori nodded. "Well, will you meet with me tomorrow and I can tell you all I've learned?"

"You betcha!" Chadwick said. "Although I doubt you'll learn *much*."

"You're probably right. But what else am I going to do on my day off?"

"Find yerself a man?"

"You sound like my friend from work, Brion." Lori rolled her eyes. "I think I need a break from dating."

"I'm kidding ya." Chadwick shrugged. "But seriously, a young girl like yerself shouldn't be spending all her free time chasing cults and demons. It's bad for your health."

Lori didn't respond. She knew he was right, but she also didn't see a better alternative.

"Well, I'll walk you back to the park."

"Yer kidding. That's a good forty minutes the opposite way you wanna go. Don't worry, lady. I'll find my own way back! You just do what you need ta do and don't worry about poor ol' Chadwick." He took another big bite from his cheese Danish.

Lori gazed off across the street. She sighed heavily. "If you insist."

"I do."

Lori scrunched her brows together. There were a few people walking up and down the street, but one had stopped. He was standing across the road, hands in the pockets of his suit jacket, eyes hidden behind foggy, gold-rimmed glasses.

He was young. His hair was blond and was swept back and combed neatly. He was handsome, too, in a boyish way.

"What's the matter?" Chadwick asked.

"Nothing. It looks like—"

The man was definitely staring at her. Intently and seriously. His mouth was a narrow and expressionless slit in his sculpted face. He didn't move. Barely seemed to be breathing.

People walked by him without a second's hesitation, as if he had both a force field and an invisible cloak around his figure.

Do I know him?

Does he recognize me?

Should I recognize him?

Why is he staring like that?

He must be aware that I see him. Why doesn't he wave or smile or—

The young man stepped off the curb and into traffic.

Lori gasped sharply, holding her hands over her mouth.

"What is it?" Chadwick asked.

A car swept toward the man. It struck him. The sound of his organic weight denting the metal hood of the Mercedes was as loud as a gunshot.

The man seemed to float in the air, his face still aimed toward Lori, before he was suddenly tugged down to the earth.

Lori watched him roll and crumble.

The car couldn't stop.

It swerved, and then its right front tire smashed into the man's cranium. It burst like a pimple. Brain matter and blood zipped across the curb and sloshed into the gutter.

Lori stood, knocking her chair down.

"What is it? Lori! Tell me!" Chadwick shouted.

The other patrons were staring. Not at the mangled body, but at Lori!

She scanned her surroundings, suddenly feeling humiliated by her honest reaction. Stuttering, she spoke, "L-look! That poor man's been hit!"

She pointed toward the road.

To her surprise, the body was getting up to its feet.

The man's head had been pulverized. All that remained was a raggedy rope of flesh and tangled musculature. Bits of golden hair hung from the end of the knotted mess, like moss growing on a wet branch.

Lori shrieked.

"Lori!" Chadwick stood and rushed to her side, holding her arm in a tight fist.

The body began to lurch toward them, taking long strides on its wobbly feet. It held its arms out ahead of it and it opened its hands into gnarled claws. She saw that his fingernails had all been broken in the collision. Some were bent back, exposing the raw bed beneath. Others were jagged shards, the shape of broken glass, and just as sharp.

This can't be happening! Lori thought, stupefied by what she was seeing.

"Lori!" Chadwick shouted, pulling her attention away from the ghoulish body. "Lori . . . the Bible is a lie. The only written word of any god is the maddening script found in *The Text of the Inninian*. Do you understand, girl? That book isn't just the answer . . . it is the *truth*!"

"Wh-what?"

Chadwick's mouth fell open. Wide open. It dropped down so low she could see the cathedral of his oral cavity. The sun's bright beams reached down and illuminated his ribbed, rippling gullet.

She tried to jerk her arm away from him, but his grip was tight. She felt attached to him!

Lori looked around, hoping for help.

Unfortunately, everyone sitting around her had died.

A woman at a table nearby was still sputtering as the last droplets of blood flowed unstaunched from her slit throat. She tilted her head back, exposing the ragged wound to the elements. It was like a delicate, frilled, pink cave.

At another table, a man's head lay on his plate. His blood mixed with his eggs—over easy.

All around her, corpses lay sprawled. Each one with a nasty wound across their throat, pouring blood, which was trickling toward her feet in trembling runnels.

Lori looked again at the road. The headless body was nearing her, his hands groping the air for her.

She turned back toward Chadwick. His transformation hadn't been completed yet. His mouth was a yawning pit, and his eyes were now glowing a bright yellow—the color of rancid piss and rotten teeth. Black ink poured out of his ears, coating his shoulders in goopy fluid. His grip continued to tighten. She could feel his nails puncturing her skin . . . digging into the flesh . . . grazing the bone.

Something came up from his throat.

It was scaly, fearsome, toothy . . . and it smelled like sun-dried fish!

Lori screeched—

—and woke up.

She was sitting at her table, looking across the street. The blond man smirked toward her, then turned and strolled merrily away.

"Lori?" Chadwick asked.

She was relieved to see his blind eyes, his white beard, and his warm smile.

"Yes?"

"You kind of trailed off there," Chadwick said. "Did something distract you?"

She didn't know how to answer him.

Her dream had felt so real. Even now, her arm tingled where the claws had scratched her.

Maybe it wasn't a dream.

Perhaps, Lori, it was a premonition.

Or a warning.

Or a summoning.

Something wants me to find out the truth. To read the book.

Or . . . it wants me to abandon my cause. It wants me to go nowhere near the book.

Either way . . . I have to read it now, don't I?

"I guess I got caught up in my own thoughts, Chaddy," Lori said. "I'm sorry. What were you saying?"

Chadwick swallowed. Even without eyesight, he could tell when he was being lied to. Lori felt her cheeks redden, but she held her hands together and waited for the moment to pass. When it did, Chadwick nodded and said, "If you say so, Lori. If you say so."

Tell him the truth.

Tell him what you saw.

Lori ignored this voice.

All she could think about was finding and reading the book. Like Eve, she was easily tempted by forbidden fruit.

The Devouring The Whore

"I WAS A LOT like you," the redheaded woman said. "I was! You don't believe me but it's true."

She scraped the edge of the knife across the mewling woman's face. The blade cut her skin easily, leaving a scarlet line from her cheekbone to the edge of her flaring nostril.

"But I changed. I changed when I met *him*."

And that was the truth. She was no longer Ulma Thompson, street whore and sad sack. She'd been transformed into a literal goddess of a religion she hadn't been aware of before now.

Ill-Et-Ellion-Inninian. Temptress of Stars. Goddess of Lust. The Unholy Whore of the Inninian Family. Devourer of Virgins.

Each title was like a powerful orgasm to her. When she thought of them, her entire body trembled.

Of all the women in the city . . . he chose me. To be his Sister-Bride. To be his co-host.

What an honor.

The physical transformation was outstanding as well. An orange glow surrounded her naked body, preternatural and flickering. As if she was a human hearth. Her teeth had fallen out and were replaced with sharper chompers. Dark, black, and tipped with sharklike needles. Her mouth was vicious and distorted. A swirling tunnel of blades and unending hunger.

And her hands.

Those had once been her breadwinners. She had soft hands, which held cocks like they'd spring away if she wasn't careful enough. Now they were weapons. Each digit was connected by a translucent web. She'd developed extra joints in every finger as well, and they were tipped with sharpened nails. Long, curved, snow-white talons that swept through flesh as easily as a machete cuts through a vine.

She was holding a homeless woman against a wall, and she was toying with her meaty subject. The woman was named Tina Rothberg—she didn't need to ask; she just *knew* this was the woman's name. She had been divorced suddenly from her husband, who'd dipped his wick into the secretary pool and decided he preferred young flesh to his wife's. Without the skills to find stable work, Tina had tried waitressing and bartending, all of which fell away from her. It had only taken her one year to be evicted and cast into the street.

Ill-Et-Ellion-Inninian licked her watery chops. Her tongue had changed as well. It was now split down the middle, like that of a reptile.

"Please!" Tina coughed. "I ain't done nuthin' to you!"

"Do you know who I am, slut?" Ill-Et-Ellion-Inninian rasped. Where once she'd had a voice like a bird's song, now she sounded like sandpaper and distorted radio transmissions. Robotic and droning.

"No! I won't tell nobody! I don't know who you are!" Tina cried.

Ill-Et-Ellion-Inninian held the tip of her knife against Tina's bouncing chin. She drove it in just enough to unleash a ribbon of blood.

"No!" Tina shouted, as if she'd been gored.

Ill-Et-Ellion-Inninian withdrew the knife. Tina whimpered with relief. She began to piss her pants. Her liquids teased Ill-Et-Ellion-Inninian's nose.

"Filthy human!" she roared.

"I'm sorry! I didn't mean to!" Tina brayed. "Please, jus' lemme go and I won't tell anyone! I promise!"

Ill-Et-Ellion-Inninian, The Concubine, seized Tina by the throat. Her nails left red grooves in the woman's unwashed flesh. The action stilled Tina's warbling voice. Her eyes expanded and her lips trembled.

"Do you realize that it is a privilege to spill blood at my altar?"

Tina didn't seem to know how to respond.

"Come with me. I'll show you Hell!" Ill-Et-Ellion-Inninian began to drag Tina down the corridor. Their scampering feet sloshed the sewer water beneath them. Tina struggled to walk straight with the demoness's hand leashed around her throat.

Tina jabbered for freedom but seemed aware of the futility of arguing with the monster. Her complaints were stifled quickly.

"The tunnels are the veins of this putrid, rotted city!" Ill-Et-Ellion-Inninian snarled. "They are its tombs as well. We are building an army, Tina Rothberg. An army to rival the populace above!"

"Please! I jus' wanna go ho-o-ome!" Tina whimpered.

"This is your home! I know all about you, Tina. I know you eat whatever you pick from garbage cans. That you've sold your mouth in exchange for narcotics! I know about the police officer who brutalized you just because he was bored, and he knew you'd never report it. I know you ride the subways most days and come here to hide when things get rough on the surface."

"Please! Let me go!" Tina screamed.

The demon laughed. It was a nasty noise that echoed through the tunnel.

She thrust Tina ahead and released her. The heavyset woman splashed face-first into the water. She could feel her hands tearing open as she tried to stop her fall. She planted her palms directly on a reef of shattered glass.

Crying, Tina scuttled up to her knees and squinted to investigate her palms. They were illuminated by the warm glow that surrounded her tormentor.

Each hand was shredded. A green shard of glass protruded like a broken bone from between the index and middle fingers of her left hand. Her palms seemed to be smiling at her through multiple crimson gashes.

"Wh-why?" Tina wheezed. 'Why are you doing this to me?"

The light was gone. Ill-Et-Ellion-Inninian had departed, leaving Tina alone in the dark.

She blinked her tears away and swallowed a rising lump of bile. Her stomach was in knots and her crotch itched. She wanted to rush through the tunnels, find a ladder, and go to the surface. She vowed to never enter the sewer system for as long as she lived.

"I didn't do nuthin' wrong," Tina bawled. "Nuthin' wrong."

She worked blindly, plucking the glass fragments out of her hands. She got the big pieces, but the little grainy particles would need tweezing.

She had never seen anything like that monster before, with her webbed hands, sharp teeth, supernatural glow.

And the creature had known so much about Tina.

How?

Tina shook her head. There would be no answering this question. The easy rationale was that she'd just encountered one of Satan's demons.

I need to go to church tomorrow.

Pray to Jesus that He'll protect me.

Hobbling forward, Tina hoped God was watching out for her. Hoped it had been His presence that had scared off the demon.

Don't question why it left, just be thankful it did.

She froze.

Ahead of her, two pinpricks of yellow light shined.

They walked toward her with a slow gait, dragging their feet through the sludge.

"Hello?" Tina whined.

The approaching figure didn't respond. It just continued toward her.

Its eyes were bright. Like two flashlights held side by side.

What on God's Earth?

A low moan issued forth from the imminent traveler.

"Wh-who are you?" Tina asked, clutching her bleeding hands together. "Please, don't hurt me. I just wanna get out of here."

The moan became louder. It sounded hollow, like a shout echoing through the hallways of a deep, dark cave.

"Leave me alone!" Tina wept.

"No!" the ghastly figure barked.

Tina twirled around and ran down the dark corridor, her feet slipping and sliding beneath her. She pinwheeled her arms and breathed heavily as she charged forward.

And then there was light.

A sudden orange brightness which almost blinded her and exposed her surroundings.

Tina wasn't alone in the sewers. And she didn't have *one* foul pursuer. She was overcrowded by fiendish ghouls, all of whom rushed toward her from the shadows, their arms extended, and their hands clawed.

Dead.

These folks are dead!

Tina wailed as she took in the appearances of her enemies. They were all rotten, most from the inside out. Their flesh clung to their narrow bodies in parchment scraps. Their eyes were hollow holes, and their mouths were lipless, exposing rows of diseased, jagged, stony teeth. Some of their mouths reminded her of angry, infected wounds, weeping fresh blood and wriggling with maggots.

They were all dressed in raggedy robes. Beige, cobwebbed, and stained. A few were naked, but they were so decayed it was impossible to tell what sex they'd been.

One of the nearest zombies grabbed her by the shoulder and held her steady. Tina was too frightened to fight back. She quivered in the brute's clutch, watching as it leered toward her. Despite its empty sockets, the thing appeared to glower at her.

Its mouth popped open, and she watched as a thick snake wriggled loose, corkscrewing around the fiend's shredded throat, then dropped like a wet tube of shit into the water. The snake slithered off, hissing mildly.

"No!" Tina cried. "No!"

The zombie leaned in and sank its teeth into Tina's cheek. With a sloppy grunt, he pulled away, tearing the flesh away from her teeth. Tina gulped and sputtered, spewing blood and screams all at once.

The creature released her, using both hands to hold her cheek meat in its chomping mouth. It ground its teeth over her flesh, causing blood to pop from its maw and tattoo her screaming face.

Tina fell back and landed on her rump. She scrambled backward, not caring that even more glass was spearing her hands. She was too distracted by the hot fire that rushed over her face.

Her tongue involuntarily investigated the wound, causing more sparks of agony. Blood pumped out of her and showered the tunnel's wall.

The zombies stumbled toward her, their grabbing arms outstretched and moaning loudly. It sounded like a choir of upset stomachs.

This can't be real!

This can't be happening!

Tina spun around, wanting to run as far and as fast as she could.

She was startled by the figure standing behind her. The twin yellow orbs in their sunken sockets. Its almond-shaped teeth. The creature took a lurching step toward her, grinning maliciously.

It was the she-demon. She'd changed even more, losing the last scraps of her humanity. Her skin seemed to be melting away from her bones. It had turned into a lumpy, gray-green porridge, which trickled away from her face and exposed the skull beneath. The claws were black and glossy, as if they were carved from pure obsidian.

Her webbed hands had cracked open, allowing longer, gleaming talons to grow from their gory centers.

The woman's vagina was swarmed with wriggling maggots. The flesh was honeycombed where the eggs had been laid and burst. The white, writhing tubes reminded Tina of stubby fingers, each one ending in a cockhead bell.

Ill-Et-Ellion-Inninian took another jaunty step forward, holding her gore-draped arms out toward Tina.

Tina felt groping hands all around her. The zombies had ambled toward her while she'd been paralyzed by fear. They had her in their grubby clutches. They did not hesitate.

She felt a clawed, rotten hand seize her throat. The nails speared her flesh and crinkled through her muscles. The hand tore sideways, ripping a hole beneath her crumpled chin. Blood hosed freely from the wound, spattering the wet floor and ejaculating from her in nasty ropes.

Another hand leapt down the front of her pants. She squirmed in place, feeling rootlike fingers curl up and plunge into her sex. The brute ripped her pussy flesh away from her pelvis in a simple tear, as if it was pulling a page from the Bible. The zombie held up the tattered strip of raw skin with curly pubes for Tina to see.

The hand closed over the meat, squeezing it like a dishcloth. Blood and strands of tattered flesh exploded from between the zombie's gray fingers.

Tina tried to scream. All she could emit was a burping chainsaw snort and a payload of fresh blood.

More hands held her.

They rucked her shirt up, exposing her pendulous breasts. She watched in horror as the zombies grappled with her mammary glands, squeezing, squelching, and spearing the pale meat.

The left breast was the first to be dug hollow. All that remained was a circlet of gaping skin and a pulpy deposit of red mesh. Fatty fluids drained down the swell of her belly and plopped into the water.

She could hear the zombies chewing on their prizes, eating her breast meat in slow, crunching, gluttonous bites.

Tina wanted to fall, but hands were supporting her. Holding her up.

And while she died, she watched the she-demon. The vile creature lingered ahead of her, enjoying the view. Languishing in Tina's spritzing blood and weak mewling.

The demoness approached. Easily and simply, she swiped her claws across Tina's belly. The skin peeled open. Loose loops of intestines spilled out of her in a curdled rush.

Tina spat a mouthful of clotted blood, then slumped into the crowd of zombies. Delicately, they lowered her to the ground and ate their fill.

And while Tina's corpse was munched into an indefinable pile of broken bones and sinewy gore, the demoness laughed . . . and laughed . . . and *laughed!*

BOOK TWO

A City of Tombs

The Vilest Principle

A Book of Unending Terror

It was just Lori's luck that she arrived at Sergio Bianchi's office just as he was returning from a lecture.

He scrutinized her quickly and frowned.

"You're not one of my students. Thinking of switching majors? Don't. There's no money in the occult."

Lori couldn't help but chuckle. "No. I'm not a student here."

"Ah. So, you're an adoring fan of my work?"

"Unfortunately, I hadn't heard about you until yesterday."

"Oh! You saw me on the tube?" Bianchi opened his office door and led the way in.

"Yes." Lori simplified things. "And I was curious to hear more about . . . what's been happening. I hope you don't mind me intruding, but I was in the area and figured I'd give it a shot."

"I appreciate it. Not many people want to stick around and hear me out. Not even during my lectures. I think some of the students attend those just to catch a nap. Nope. Unless you're into strict satanism, the obscure occult bears little to no interest to most laypeople nowadays."

Lori looked around his office. It was small and cramped, and he'd cluttered it with artifacts. Some looked like tacky figurines he'd procured from tourist traps. Others were more elaborate. Like the tentacled beings of stones that sat in a neat row along the edge of his desk. Or the handwoven tapestry, which depicted a snarling wolf with a halo made of sunbeams, chomping down on a pyramid with a gleaming, tear-stained eye at its center.

There were African masks, crystal pendants, and little sculptures of alien beings.

Even his calendar expressed his singular interest. On its top page was the design of an ancient rune.

"What book do you have there?"

"Oh, this?" Lori held up the tome. "I bought it today."

"*Cults and Their Practices*?"

"Yes."

"It's a decent beginner's guide, but it's *very* surface level."

"You've read it?"

"Yes. Back in college and once again recently, before I donated it to my favorite bookstore."

"Morty's?"

"That's the one."

"Well, that's where I got it. This is probably your copy!"

"I'd bet it is." Bianchi showed his teeth. "Why don't you have a seat, Ms.—"

"Lyric. Lori Lyric."

She sat on the rickety chair across from him, like a student in the principal's office. Bianchi knit his chubby fingers over his chest and tilted back in his reclining chair. He looked tired, with his puffy eyes, his unshaven face, and his warty complexion. He smelled like sweat and his shirt had food stains.

He's probably a little mad.

Has to be, if he's invested so much of himself into—

Lori coughed. "Well, this is what brought me here. I went to Morty's hoping to find something—anything—about the Inninian."

Bianchi brightened. "Well, you came to the right place."

"I'm trying to work out the link between the cult and . . . some things I heard from a friend of mine."

Lori explained what Chadwick had told her. She mentioned The Young Prince. At the utterance of the moniker, Bianchi scowled deeply. His expression worried her, as if she'd said something offensive at a fancy dinner. She continued through, informing Bianchi about the violence that had plagued the homeless community and how they'd drawn a link to the cult even before Bianchi had gone on the air.

"And how did they even know about the Inninian?" Bianchi asked.

"I think this . . . Young Prince is spreading the word. Like a missionary."

Lori then described her voyage to Morty's and the rumors of a translation by one Tanner Fishman—

Bianchi cut her off. "I know the boy. He and The Young Prince are one and the same. And you're right. He's the one spreading the word of *The Text of the Inninian*."

"How do you know?" Lori asked.

"Because . . . until he went mad . . . Tanner Fishman was my favorite student."

Bianchi gulped. The air seemed to have turned sour.

"I'm sorry, Ms. Lyric. But you might have just dragged yourself into a living nightmare simply by speaking his name. I'm now going to work under the assumption that you have an open mind and that you don't need to be belittled with sugarcoated realism. Am I correct in this assumption?"

"You know, if you'd asked me that this morning, I would have affirmed my skepticism. But . . . after I bought this book, I've been experiencing strange things. No. It happened before I bought this book. It happened last night."

"What did?"

"I thought I was going crazy, but last night . . . I saw a corpse. It was standing across the road, watching me. And its eyes were, well, they were glowing. A bright yellow. Like flashlight beams."

"Jesus Christ!" Bianchi yelped.

"What?"

"That was Tanner Fishman you saw."

"The Young Prince?" Lori cocked her head. "I saw him again today. I saw a vision of a handsome man with glasses being struck by a car."

"That was him too." Bianchi held his head in his hands. "But why is he making himself known to *you*?"

"I don't know," Lori said. "I hadn't even heard of this Inninian business until you spoke about it on our program. And now . . . now it's all I can think of."

Bianchi rubbed his eyes. "I guess I must tell you all I know. Otherwise, it would be like throwing you into the ocean without a life preserver."

"Am I in danger?" Lori asked.

"Yes. Grave danger. Ms. Lyric, this is not something I expect you to believe right away. Even with what you've seen, it's absurd to think you'll buy it immediately. But the Inninian are *true gods.*"

Lori was surprised that she *did* believe.

"I keep the book on my person at all times now. It's too dangerous to lend out. Maybe even too dangerous to read. I learned that the hard way when I gave poor Tanner my copy."

"What happened?" Lori asked.

"Yes. Might as well start from the beginning, shouldn't I? It's a story I haven't told before. I doubted it would be believed. Hell, I still worry you'll start laughing and calling me mad. But you are in danger. Serious danger. Unnatural danger. And the cause is Tanner Fishman."

Bianchi cleared his throat and sat up straight.

"Tanner was my brightest student last year. A wise kid. Something of a smart aleck, but there was an odd sense of charm to his japes. The kid read like a scholar and spoke like one too. Everything he said . . . it came off as if it'd been pre-prepared. Naturally, he wasn't popular with his peers. They bullied him for his intellect and his tenacity. I heard that a few boys stripped him and rushed him naked through the girls' locker room once. It'd mortified him so much he'd missed three days of classes, locking himself away in his dorm.

"Tanner took a shine to my class. He wasn't religious, but he was fascinated by the supernatural and the occult. He said it was scientific to him—only it was a science based in unfounded science. I admired his outlook and took every chance I could to encourage him. I shared books with him, gave him personal lessons, and we even practiced Magick together. Not the sort of

Magick you see in a sideshow, no. We worked with chemistry and ritualism. We used chalk to draw divine sigils, chants to incite hallucinations, and even smoke to go on inward spiritual journeys.

"He was the only student who treated my work with any seriousness. I must admit, it made me swoon. In an academic manner, of course."

Whatever you say, Lori thought, recalling how even Plato had been lecherous toward his young, intellectually stimulating students.

"Anyway, he became fascinated with dead and lost cults. I stoked his fervor by sharing what books I had on the subject. He read them voraciously. I asked Tanner what it was that drew him toward such subjects, and he told me this, 'It's forbidden fruit. Like discovering a color you haven't seen before. Thinking a thought that feels original. Tasting something that damages your tongue forever.' He was a very eloquent speaker."

More like pretentious. Lori held in a giggle.

"The Inninian became his obsession. He found out about them through that book you have there. Here, pass it to me. I'll read the passage to you."

Bianchi scrolled through the pages before landing toward the book's end. He coughed before reading aloud, "*Stranger still are the 'unpronounceable' cults. Cults whose very languages have gone extinct, as have their practices. Take, for instance, the Inninian.*

Only a few copies of their holy text exist. Most others were burned in the Crusades by a different sort of cult entirely. Christianity." Bianchi shut the book. "And then it goes on about the Crusades."

Wow. Ten bucks for all that information. Gee. What a bargain. Lori knew Morty wouldn't give her a refund, but maybe she could pawn the book off somewhere.

"Tanner asked me about the Inninian, and I was quick to share with him my rare copy of their bible. I told him little was known about them, only the facts I mentioned on the news yesterday. You remember?"

"That they are reported to be prehuman? That their language is untranslatable? And that they have diagrams of violent rituals?"

"Yes. That about covers it. Anyway, I let Tanner have the book. He'd won me over with his enthusiasm. He went off, happy to be carrying it. Then, he came back the next day—"

Bianchi shuddered.

Lori felt a draft herself. She hugged her unhelpful book to her bosom.

"The next day . . . he'd changed. He brought the book back to me. But he was carrying a notebook with him, which was filled with scribbles. There was something wrong with him. His flesh was pale and tacky. His eyes were bright—and I'm telling the truth—yellow. Almost glowing around their ridges. And he smiled at me and proudly tossed his notes onto my desk, saying, 'I translated it last night.' I, of course, wanted to laugh. Thinking he'd played an awful joke on me. I chided him, but he grew dead serious and told me, 'No. I translated the book. This is the very first English translation.' I frowned and said something along the lines of: How? The language is long lost. It may even be gibberish. You're a bright kid, Tanner, but there's no way you could have translated this book. No way at all. And then he looked angry. He snarled at me. Literally. Like a rabid dog. Then he snatched up his notebook and spat on my desk. I was just about to scold him when he shouted, 'I was given visions! Such sweet, beautiful, nightmarish visions!' He left, raving nonsense. Speaking in a language I did not recognize." Bianchi shook his head. "I think it was—as hard as this is to believe—the language from *The Text of the Inninian*."

The professor let this statement sit in the air above him.

"Or it was madness. I can't tell for sure. But it was . . . awfully close to the opening passage of the book. That passage is believed to be the 'Family Tree' of the Inninian gods. Here, I'll show you."

Bianchi was on his feet and waddling. He plucked an ancient tome from his satchel and set it in Lori's hands.

"This is the book?" Lori asked in disbelief.

"Yes. Whether it's priceless or worthless, no one seems to be able to tell. But open it and you'll see."

Lori opened the book and found the very first page was filled with strange runes and letters."

"This is, of course, not an original. According to testimony, the *actual* bibles were burned. It was only a few vague 'reprints' that survived, and as you can see . . . the effort to translate was fruitless."

Lori studied the page. The letters and words and incongruous text irritated her eyes and itched her brain. But there was, indeed, a family tree. And it looked like this.

Annon-Et-Elliph-Inninian beget
Upsure-Ollion-Iän-Inninian beget
Ulpher-Bannon-Gepth-Inninian beget
Pharsher-Tolen-Yllin-Inninian beget
The Foul Twins, Barsipher-Maagrer-Et-Inninian and Ill-Et-Ellion-Inninian, whose union birthed the Reya-Et-Ettphiliophis-Inninian.

"And trust me, this is the most legible segment of the book. Turn the page."

Lori did so and felt as if she'd been punched in the face. It was a mess of letters, both English and bizarre. Runes, sketches, and squiggly lines decorated the page, almost overcrowding each other for attention.

"My God!" Lori said. "This *is* impossible to translate. So . . . how did Tanner do it?"

"I used to think he didn't. I think he went mad and wrote—I dunno—a political and spiritual manifesto? It incites violence, whatever he wrote. And it's tied directly to what he *thinks* he read in this book. But then . . . the nightmares started. Dreams and visions, much like the ones you experienced today. I saw living corpses shambling through our city. Tearing through the flesh of the living. I saw demons overtaking innocent bodies—breaking them. I saw them. The Inninian. Horrible creatures. Gods, yes . . . but not benevolent. I saw that one had possessed Tanner—a younger god named Barispher, one of The Foul Twins. I saw him summoning his sister to overtake a street whore. I saw the two laughing together as they bled human beings like stuck pigs! These visions assaulted me, day and night. Tormented me. I saw Hell, Ms. Lyric. I saw *Hell*."

Bianchi took a long, juddering breath. He'd worked himself into a frenzy. His cheeks were red, and his eyes were watery. He dabbed at his face with a handkerchief. "I'm sorry. I haven't been believed yet and . . . and I can tell you believe me. You already know just how evil this is."

Lori nodded in agreement. "I'm not sure if I *believe* it, but I do *know* it."

"For me, that's enough!" Bianchi sighed and sat down heavily.

"Why didn't you tell the police?"

"I did. They didn't believe me. Thought I was the mad one. And when I went on your news program. I proved them right. I didn't want to believe it was Tanner. I wanted to think it was a different nutcase who'd started the cult up again. That was, until I heard about the ritual performed in the hairdresser's shop."

Bianchi took the book, flipped through the pages, then showed Lori a full-page illustration.

"This ritual."

"What is it supposed to accomplish?" Lori asked.

"I haven't the faintest clue. But I know it can only get worse . . . before it becomes truly awful."

Lori felt something *plop* onto her shoulder. She about shrieked when she turned her head and saw a curling slug resting there. Yipping, she batted it off of her. It splatted on the floor, oozing mucus and wheezing loudly.

"What was that?" Bianchi asked.

"A disgusting creature! A slug!" Lori shouted.

Another slug landed in her hair.

Lori was quick to pluck it and toss it. This cigar-sized gastropod landed on the desk. It formed a *U* shape and squealed like bacon on a hot skillet. She watched as a gushing rush of fluid stained Bianchi's unorganized papers.

"What the hell?" Bianchi asked.

Both of them turned their heads up. They gasped in collective shock.

The ceiling was crawling with slugs. Their fibrous, warty bodies rustled together as they squirmed, slithered, and secreted. Long tubes of lubricant dangled like clear stalactites from the ceiling, dribbling onto the floor and Lori's lap. The sound of squelching was like pulped fruit being squeezed in angry fists.

She jerked herself upright, turned, and raced to the door. She gripped the knob and yanked, only to be dismayed by its immobility. The door was welded shut. It didn't even jitter in its frame.

"The key!" she cried. "Unlock this door!"

Another slug dropped from the ceiling. It hit the floor like a mound of cow dung. Lori could feel its mucus speckling her ankles.

Bianchi huffed his way over to the door. "Pull it! It pulls!"

"I *am* pulling!" Lori responded. "Just unlock it!"

Bianchi grabbed the knob and tugged. He pulled hard enough to have jerked it off its hinges.

The door didn't even shake!

Is this another vision? Lori wondered. *Because this feels as real as the last one did! Even more real!*

She looked up at the ceiling. The slugs were moving in an undulating wave. More of them dropped and splattered, each one bigger and squirmier than the last. Some were the size of bratwurst. Others were thicker, bulgier, and veinier. Like disconnected cocks, crawling down toward her—stiff and ready to rape!

Oh God. Get me out of here!

She took the knob and jerked on it desperately, pushing Bianchi aside.

"Where did they come from?" he screamed.

"I don't know!"

"It has to be Tanner. It has to be!" Bianchi cried. "Oh God. He's punishing me for opening my mouth on the news! This has to be Tanner!"

"Shut up!" Lori screeched. "Help me get this door open!"

A slug slapped her back. She whirled, clawing behind her. Her nails dug into the slug flesh. The creature burst like a water balloon filled with chunky soup. She drew her hands back and looked at her digits with wide-eyed horror. Each sticky finger was stained piss-yellow and snot-green.

Bianchi continued to struggle with the door. He was gibbering weakly, his heart overloading with panic.

He's going to drop dead if he isn't careful!

She couldn't imagine being stuck in this room alone.

It sounded like the slugs were chewing. All around her, it sounded like splintering wood and grinding metal.

"Let me out! Tanner! Tanner! I'm sorry!" Bianchi cried. "I'm so sorry!"

The door fell open.

Bianchi shouted with relief—

—before the gloved hand shot out of the darkness and grabbed him by his ample throat, cutting his noises off.

Bianchi opened his mouth to scream. All that came out was a raspy wheeze.

"Suffer!" an angry voice screeched. "Suffer!"

Lori planted her hands against her cheeks and yowled, backing into the farthest corner.

She watched in horror as the intruder shoved Bianchi to the ground. He squirmed and barked, but he was quickly pinned.

The assailant was young. Handsome. Blond. His eyes were obscured behind his glasses. His black leather gloves shimmered as if they were wet.

He held Bianchi's head down with his right hand while the left swept behind him and dug into his back pocket.

"Let him go!" Lori shouted, finding her courage.

The slugs were gone. They'd disappeared the second this heinous intruder had appeared, as if they had been an illusion after all.

Lori couldn't rationalize it. The bizarre reality she'd stumbled into was too hostile and fast-moving for consideration.

Tanner—it had to be him—yanked an implement out from his back pocket. It was metallic, pear-shaped, and so rusted it looked bloodstained. She saw that at its top where it thinned out, there sat a golden spigot.

Bianchi kept his mouth open, breathlessly hoping for a chance to howl.

"Suffer, nonbeliever!" Tanner snarled.

He slammed the bottom of the metallic pear into Bianchi's mouth.

Lori heard his teeth shatter and his gums rip. Loops of blood exploded from his maw and draped his wobbling chin. Bianchi pinched his eyes shut and tensed up, his pain crippling and automatic.

Tanner stirred the pear, driving it down deeper into Bianchi's oral cavity. More blood spumed from the poor man, staining Tanner's black gloves. Making them even more glittery and moist.

Lori didn't want to look, but she couldn't draw her eyes away.

One more shove put the pear so far into Bianchi's mouth, his throat began to balloon.

Tanner grabbed the spigot . . . and began to turn it.

The pear opened up like a flower. There were four segments, which creaked loudly as they broke apart, splitting Bianchi's mouth.

His eyes bugged out of their sockets. Twin streams of blood hosed from his flared nostrils. He could no longer scream. He began, instead, to weep.

Another turn and Lori could hear the professor's jawbone splinter, shatter, and spear through his mushy flesh.

Another turn.

Another.

The pear was spread wide, distorting Bianchi's facial features. His cheeks were rumpled like a wet bath mat. His lower jaw cracked downward. Blood was pouring from every available orifice.

Lori could smell filth crawling out of Bianchi's bowels.

Tanner grabbed the spigot with his fingers. With a heaving grunt, he yanked it free. It came loose with a sloshy eruption of blood and clinging gore. Scraps of tissue held onto the nasty edges of the opened pear. Gurgling emissions filled the office like a bad smell. Bianchi began to seize up, his limbs rattling and his head knocking up and down. As if he was trying to dance his way out of his agony.

Tanner looked at Lori.

Behind his glasses, his eyes were glowing a sadistic shade of yellow. It reminded her of the eyes of a hungry feline and a crafty reptile.

He held the dribbling, metallic pear toward her. She watched as ribbons of blood fell from its slices and dotted the floor.

Bianchi jarringly froze. His eyes had turned white. Everything below his nose and above his clavicle was broken.

Tanner stood up. His grin didn't waver.

"You, Lori, will join our ranks! You will be a helpful servant, won't you?"

She didn't know how to respond. His voice was so calm and cool, as if he hadn't just committed an atrocious murder.

I just watched someone die.

Holy Christ!

I SAW SOMEONE DIE!

Lori wished she could faint, but she was too frightened. She feared the darkness just as much as she feared Tanner Fishman. It zapped her into a state of total awareness.

She could smell the blood. Could hear the last bits of gas escape Bianchi's corpse. Could even taste the hot tang of death!

Just as it overwhelmed her—

—Lori woke up.

She was being reassured by a calm voice.

"You all right, ma'am?"

Lori blinked. Her surroundings were fuzzy, but the man who was kneeling by her seemed sturdy and gentle. He was Hispanic, muscled, and handsome. He wore all white—like an angel!

"Hu-huh?" Lori muttered.

"Hey. Easy. You've had quite a shock. You screamed before you fainted. Loud enough to draw attention. They found you on the floor and Professor Bianchi—"

"Is he dead?" Lori sputtered. "Did that really happen?"

"I'm afraid so."

"Oh God!" Lori proclaimed. "All that blood!"

"Blood?" the man asked.

"Yes! Oh, it was terrible!"

"You must still be confused, ma'am. Professor Bianchi . . . he died of a heart attack?"

Lori looked flummoxed.

"Yes. Must've happened right in front of you. Gave you a huge shock. But we did a quick exam. Doesn't look like you hit your head when you fainted. Still, we'd like to take you in for observation."

"I'm sorry. What?" Lori's face was pale.

She realized where she was. She'd been brought into the hallway outside Bianchi's office. Two paramedics came out from the room, wheeling the professor's corpse. He was hidden beneath a white sheet, but there was no blood staining the fabric.

A heart attack? But I saw what happened! I saw what Tanner Fishman did to him!

"What's your name?" the man asked.

Lori drifted away from him, slumping down into the stiff seat she'd been propped up in.

"Your name?"

"Lori," she responded. "I'm Lori Lyric."

"I'm Samson Aldridge. Here, did you want to keep your book?"

"Book?"

"You were holding it pretty tight when we found you. I left it in the office, but I could get it for you."

Lori nodded.

When Samson returned, he was holding *The Text of the Ininian.*

Pieces on a Chessboard

"Thought you'd never show!" Whistler said.

"Takes me a while to get around," Chadwick said as he used his cane to find his seat. He grunted, cracked his knuckles, then swept his hands over the chessboard, feeling his pieces. "You gonna play fair this time?"

"I ain't promising that." Whistler snickered.

The two men fell into easy conversation while they played. They'd long ago used chalk to write letters and numbers onto the squares, and Chadwick would let his partner know where he wanted his pieces moved. Despite his joking, Whistler was always honest and put the pieces exactly where Chadwick desired. Even if it meant Whistler lost many of their games.

"Yer a sharp old coot!" Whistler snarked when Chadwick called checkmate.

"Just lucky."

Whistler set about rearranging the board.

The pieces were made of stone, as was the table they were played on. The chess boards had been implemented a long while back. Even before Whistler and Chadwick had become park regulars. Some of the pieces were missing, so Whistler had to keep track with different colored stones he kept in his backpack.

Whistler was his actual name. Paul St. Peter Whistler. He'd been homeless ever since he'd been introduced to heroin. His arms were scarred almost black, and his teeth had rotted out of his mouth. And yet, Whistler had a sunny disposition and outlook. He was always reassuring Chadwick that things could only get better from here.

"Baghead struck again," Whistler said, intruding on Chadwick's calculations.

Chadwick frowned. They'd all been aware of the rapist who'd turned the city park into his hunting ground. He sprayed his victims with mace, wrapped their heads in plastic bags, and abused them. Some even claimed to have witnessed his crimes from a distance, but no two viewers seemed to have the same description of the perpetrator.

"He was seven feet tall. Had hair down to his ass. And a hook for a hand!"

"Nah! I saw him jus' two nights ago! He was fat as a pig. 'Bout four hundred pounds! And he had a cleft lip!"

"Yer fulla it. I saw him just last night. You wouldn't believe it, but the fucker is an honest-to-God midget. And he dresses like a clown too!"

Ridiculous stories. Chadwick knew that the fiend would be disappointingly average when he eventually got caught. Maybe he'd be a tubby forty-year-old who lived with his mom after his divorce, and he resented both his mother and his ex-wife enough to blame *all* women for his woes.

Or he had no motive. He was just a freak without a leash to hold him back.

Here I go. Making stories of my own. Ho hum.

Whistler went first. In no time at all, they were halfway through an intense game. A few other folks hovered nearby, watching the competition. Whistler could see their leering faces, but Chadwick relied on their smells and noises. The scent of sweat and the rumbling of hungry tummies.

Maybe I should bring Whistler over to meet Lori. She's generous. She'll make sure he gets a meal.

Don't push it.

She'll regret helping you if you come back with all yer friends, and all of Whistler's friends, and all of Whistler's friends' friends.

"You think they'll ever catch him?" Whistler asked.

"Baghead? Maybe. I wouldn't be surprised if the cops were staking out the park. Probably sending a lady cop out each night to act like bait."

Whistler grunted. "He hasn't raped anyone wealthy yet. Don't think they'll do nuthin' until he does. What do you think a guy like that is like?"

"Gonna be just an average Joe. He'll look like you or me."

"Hopefully not. I may not be God's favorite angel, but I hope I got nuthin' in common with that scumbag."

Chadwick swirled his tongue from one cheek to the other. "I worry 'bout Lori. She lives on her own, ya know? And she's got some serious creeps in that building with her."

"Maybe one of 'em is Baghead!"

"Don't even joke about that!"

"Heard you spent the night in her place."

"Word travels fast."

"Y'all do anything fun?"

"No. She was just bein' nice and getting me outta the rain." Chadwick blushed. "I slept on her sofa and went to breakfast with her. That's it. Can't a lady be nice ta an old man without folks assumin' we doin' the dirty?"

"I'm just messing with you, old-timer. No need to get flustered and shit."

"Well, Lori's been nicer to me than just about anyone in this blasted city. You be respectful when you talk about—"

Gunshots rang out like firecrackers. They snapped across the park, muting Chadwick and hammering his ears into his cranium. He twirled in his seat, as if he could suddenly see and he wanted to get a look at the shooter.

He tasted something hot and tangy.

Blood.

People were screaming.

Whistler grabbed Chadwick and hefted him out of his seat.

"Run, old man! Run!" Whistler shouted.

Their chess game was forgotten.

Cannibal Apocalypse

Whistler panted heavily as he dragged the blind man beside him. He hadn't seen the shooter, but he'd heard the bastard!

He glanced around, watching out for danger. The park was overgrown and ill-maintained. The killer could've been hiding just about anywhere.

He'd seen the bullet slip through the body of a lady standing near Chadwick watching their game and eavesdropping on their discussion. She'd been old, gnarled, and gray-skinned. The bullet had split her chest open, as if she'd been cleaved by an ax.

She sprayed blood all over Chadwick before flopping onto the ground.

Someone screamed.

Another bullet smashed through the air and struck a young man between his eyes. Whistler watched in horror as his brains spun out of his fractured skull and painted the chessboard scarlet.

Whistler had worked fast to get to his feet and drag Chadwick away. They were surrounded by running, shouting, panicking people.

More gunshots rang out, but none seemed to find their marks.

Whistler was packed with clothes. He always wore fur coats, a fur hat, and fur mittens. Even when it was hot and sunny out. He seemed totally sane otherwise, but even he couldn't explain his aversion to regular clothing and short sleeves.

He'd been homeless for so long, he barely remembered what a warm bed felt like. Much less a peaceful night of sleep. And ever since he'd witnessed the craziness in the alley between the crucified woman and Bark, he'd been too nervous to let his guard down. Now that he and his pal were being shot at, it just confirmed his paranoia!

Christ. If we get through this, Chadwick, I'll buy you and me a great big house with triple locks on each and every door.

"My cane!" Chadwick grunted.

"No time! We'll get you a new 'un if it's not there later! C'mon! We gotta move!"

"Who's shootin'?" Chadwick wasn't able to move very fast. Whistler could almost hear the old man's bones creaking and groaning.

Whistler glanced over his shoulder and observed the hellish landscape behind him.

The shooter was standing on top of a knoll, holding a hunting rifle in her delicate hands. She was bald, wore an orange vest, and was naked below the waist. Her vagina had been mutilated. Meat hung from between her legs like shredded mozzarella.

She do that to herself?

I'll bet she did.

She looks nuts!

She held up her rifle and fired into the escaping crowd. Whistler heard someone yelp before smacking the grassy ground. The person was trampled. The sound was like a sloppy mouth chewing on pebbles and marbles.

She snapped another round in the chamber in a jerky motion, then hefted the gun up and put another victim in her sights.

Whistler ducked just in time. The bullet plowed through the top of his fur cap, sending muskrat hair everywhere.

She was gonna kill me fer nuthin'! Doesn't even know my name an' she wants me dead! Oh man! Oh God!

Whistler pulled Chadwick down into the bushes. Chadwick yelled as his legs slipped out from under him. Whistler dragged him to safety, leaving trenches in the wet earth.

"We gotta hide, bud!" Whistler said.

"Who is it?"

"Some crazy skinhead bitch! Looks like she's gone off her rocker! Maybe drugs! I dunno! Her pussy is all fucked-up! Like, shredded an' shit!"

"Why's she shootin' at us?"

"How am I supposed ta know? Shit! Yer just lucky I didn't leave your ass!"

Chadwick paused. "Thank you."

"No problem. Just return the favor someday, huh?"

"You got it."

Whistler army crawled toward the edge of the bushes. He snuck a quick glance around.

The woman had stepped off the knoll, leaving her rifle behind.

"What's she doin'?" Chadwick asked.

"I don't know. I'm watchin' her."

Most of the people had vanished, aside from those who'd been shot or injured. Whistler saw an older man crawling on his hands and knees, leaving a carpet of blood behind him. He'd been shot in the hip and blood seemed to be pissing from the wound.

The woman approached the old man silently and curiously. Like a cat stalking an ignorant lizard.

"What's happening now?" Chadwick asked impatiently.

"Shush!" Whistler hissed.

The woman grabbed the man by his white hair and held his head up. The man was crying, his mouth wide and his eyes sealed behind a layer of rubbery tears. Yellow snot oozed from his nostrils.

The woman hunkered down and clamped her mouth against the side of his throat. Even from this distance, Whistler could hear her teeth sinking in.

"Oh God!" Whistler said. "Oh God. She's eatin' him!"

She tore her head away, ripping a hunk of flesh out of the man's throat. There was a rush of red, and then Whistler spotted a flexing white tube in the center of the crater. The man burbled and choked but seemed incapable of speech.

The woman released him. He plopped onto the ground with a snorting cough. His limbs trembled, then he lay still.

She chewed him up and killed him.

Good Lord.

When will this craziness ever end?

The bald woman with mutilated genitals went over to the next survivor. A homeless woman Whistler vaguely recognized. She was short and round, and he could never tell how old she was. She was built like a child, but her face was wrinkled like she'd been stuck in a sauna for two days straight. She was Asian and spoke only a little English.

"Please!" the homeless woman brayed. "Please!"

The woman knelt down beside her and took her hand. She lifted it up and bit into her bare wrist.

Each tooth was like a knife, searing through the skin and digging into the gristle beneath. Blood hosed from the screaming lady and coated the bald woman's gruesome face.

"What's happenin'?" Chadwick asked.

"She's biting them! She's biting them!" Whistler susurrated.

"It's another ritual," Chadwick moaned.

"Shut up."

The woman stood and walked over to the next body. This one was stone-cold dead. A man who'd been trampled beneath the stomping crowd. His face looked like a crushed tin can and his left arm was a crooked protrusion.

The woman dug her fingers into his gut and pulled it open. The flesh parted way too easily.

She sank her hands into his center and upheaved a knotted rope of purple tissue. With an expression of pure ecstasy, she began to chew on the human tubing. Blood oozed out of the organs, spilling down her slick hunting jacket and spattering the ground.

"What the fuck?" Whistler breathed.

She stood, hauling the intestines with her. They snapped loudly, spurting pods of pus, streams of blood, and chunks of digested slop.

She munched loudly on the matter, closing her eyes and devoting herself to the warm mush.

"That's the sickest thing I've ever seen," Whistler said. "Be glad yer blind, man."

"What's she doing? Still eatin' on 'em?"

"Yep. Like she's at a buffet!"

"Why's she doin' that?" Chadwick muttered. "It ain't right! Ain't right!"

The woman froze in place. She was now standing near the chess table. The pieces had been scattered and the board was stained with brain curds.

She laid the coiled loops of intestines on the surface. She fashioned them into a mound, then stepped back and held her hands toward the heavens. Tilting her head back, she shouted out in a clear voice, "Brother and Sister! Accept my pledge and sacrifice!"

"What the hell?" Chadwick said.

"I dunno. She must've cracked."

The woman got down on her knees and continued to speak. "I give you flesh! I offer you blood! Accept me into your ranks! Please!"

A young man appeared behind her.

"Where'd he come from?" Whistler asked.

"Who?" Chadwick mumbled.

"Young guy. I swear to God he wasn't there a second before. Now he's right behind her!"

"What's he look like?" Chadwick asked.

"Blond. Wearin' glasses and . . . black leather gloves! Looks like a kid. Skinny guy."

Chadwick seemed to sink into the ground. "The Young Prince."

"Nah. Can't be him. That's jus' a legend."

"It's true."

"No. The people who worship this shit are just crazy. They made it all up."

"That's him. Can't you feel it? The air has changed. It feels hotter than it was a few seconds ago."

Whistler had to admit that he was sweating beneath his furs. The air felt the same as it did around a stagnant pond. One filled with dead fish and so murky that you couldn't see what was lurking beneath its still waters.

He looked back out at the guy. If it was indeed The Young Prince, then he was beautiful. His face was chiseled and firm, and his skin seemed to glow in the sun.

Another figure appeared in front of the woman. This person was less favorable.

It looked like a troll.

A female body, with breasts and a cup of hairy flesh between her limber legs. She looked aquatic, with webbed hands, gills, and yellow eyes that seemed to pop out of their sockets. Her mouth was filled with razor fangs.

A mutant!

The creature opened its mouth and unleashed a raspy howl.

The blood-soaked woman covered her face and began to cry.

The Young Prince grabbed her by the base of her neck and lifted her to her feet. The woman squirmed in his grip, like a kitten held by its scruff.

"Let me go!" the woman cried. "Please! I didn't know! I didn't know!"

The creature raked its claws across the woman's exposed pelvis, unzipping the flesh beneath the swell of her tummy. Pulpy guts and knots of gore streamed from the hole and spilled onto the ground.

The Young Prince tossed her body away. Red streamers followed it like ribbons attached to a flying kite.

"They killed her," Whistler rasped.

"Who? The cops?"

"No. The monsters!"

The mutant and The Young Prince both turned toward Whistler. Their motions were jarring and frightening. Whistler felt his heart fill his throat and pump through his cranium. His mouth went dry, and his eyes turned wet.

"Oh God," Whistler said. "They're lookin' at me."

"We should run."

"I don't think we can. They came outta nowhere. I don't think they travel like regular folk."

"What should we do?"

"I dunno. Pray?"

Whistler blinked.

The two fiends were closer to him now. In that single moment, they'd come halfway from the chess table to the bushes.

They had company.

Three skeletal figures stood by them, wavering in place like scarecrows in a windy field. They were toothy, festering with maggots, and their skin was so dehydrated it fell from their bones in bacon-thick flakes. The zombies made no noise. They were like disintegrating mannequins.

Whistler blinked again.

The Young Prince and the mutant were both gone. Now there were six zombies in total. Some were nude, others wore potato-sack-colored robes.

Whistler stood and ran.

"Whistler!" Chadwick shouted.

Whistler didn't care. Moments ago, he'd considered Chadwick his closest friend. Now, he hoped that the blind and helpless man would provide an adequate distraction.

They'll be so busy feasting on him . . . I'm just gonna get away! Get away and never come back!

I'll leave this crazy city. I'll go somewhere peaceful, where nobody gets shot, crucified, or gutted by mutants! I'll go somewhere—

Whistler broke out of the park and found himself scrambling across the street. He must have looked crazy to those passing by. A dude wearing nothing but pelts, running like a bat out of hell! Well, he didn't care how he looked.

All he wanted to do was run.

Love Hate

Kern opened the door and wasn't at all surprised to see Patsy standing on the other side. She gave him a smile and got on her tiptoes, planting a wet kiss on his cracked lips.

"Surprise!" she said as she made her way past him and into his apartment. She carried a sack of groceries with her, which she set on his kitchen counter.

She looked pretty. Her brown hair was tied back, and her face was made up. Even though she was dressed casually, Kern knew she was hoping he'd see sparks when he looked at her.

"Hey. What's up?" He put his hands in the pockets of his tight jeans. There was a substantial lump at the crotch that trickled down his left thigh. He knew she liked these jeans, but he didn't always wear them just for her.

He wasn't wearing anything else. His hairy chest was sheened with sweat. He'd been masturbating before Patsy had knocked.

Kern wondered if she could smell the pre-ejaculate oozing from his slit.

"I came by last night, but your neighbor said you'd gone out. Hope it wasn't with another girl." Patsy laughed nervously.

She's so insecure.

Good.

Kern scoffed. "Nah. Had some creative blockage to work through. Figured a late-night beer run would do the trick, only I wound up at some dive bar. Drank a bit too much, so don't yell, okay?"

"Like this?" Patsy shouted.

Kern pretended to flinch and cover his ears.

Patsy grinned. "I won't do that again. Just figured I owed you for leaving me high and dry last night."

"Well, if you had called ahead, I would've stuck around." Kern walked over and wrapped his arms around her. "That prick next door give you much trouble?"

"No. I mean, he did his usual spiel. Told me he'd make me a star." Patsy rolled her eyes. "How do you live next to someone like that?"

"I'll wring his scrawny neck one of these days."

"I don't think he's worth the trouble," Patsy said.

They kissed again. He knew he was musky and slick. She was soft and squishy. When their lips separated, he gave her a wink. "Hey. Wanna do it?"

"You're so romantic," Patsy said. "Lemme make us something to eat first. That's why I came over."

Before long, she was serving him a rare steak and a baked potato with bacon bits, sour cream, and chives. They both ate happily.

"So, you come up with something after your walkabout?"

"Not really." Kern frowned. "Maybe I'm not cut out for this artsy fartsy stuff."

He'd convinced Patsy that he was a poet. The truth was, he'd rewrite poems he read from library books and pass them off to her as his own. So far, the ruse had kept her fooled.

"Well, one bad night shouldn't sink your ship. You just gotta relax for a while. Maybe find some inspiration," Patsy said.

"You're probably right. You know how I am, though. My own worst critic."

"Well, I ain't gonna let you quit easy." Patsy scarfed down a mouthful of potato.

"Maybe I should break up with you."

"Har-har."

She knew he was joking, and yet her face was still briefly scrunched with concern. He liked that. Liked keeping her on edge. Liked when she worried.

Stupid bitch.

Kern laughed off the joke and went back to cutting the fat off of his steak. He ate it afterward. Even the gristle.

With their dirty dishes in the sink, Kern corralled Patsy into his bedroom. He tore her clothes away, like an animal ripping the flesh off of a bloated corpse. He gnawed on her nipples, swirling them with his tongue and nipping at them with his teeth. Each bite caused Patsy to gasp and shiver. He could feel goose pimples blooming on her arms. He could also feel her growing wet down below. He prodded her entrance with his staff, enjoying the way her flesh tickled his stern muscle.

"Wait! Alex! What about protection?"

He didn't respond. He moved up and latched his mouth on the side of her throat. He inhaled. Deeply. She writhed and mewled, enjoying the suction.

I could swallow you whole, Kern thought as he pushed his prick into her tunnel.

Her muscles seized, closing around him like a moist fist. And that just made it all the better! He tugged back and forth, filling and voiding her in quick rhythms.

"Oh, Alex. Yes, Alex. Yes," she moaned.

He closed his eyes.

Remembered the bitch he'd bashed last night in the park.

She'd screamed so loud when he shoved himself inside.

He'd actually been worried. There was no way that noise had gone unheard. He had imagined flashing red and blue lights. Public humiliation. Maybe he'd be executed, even though he hadn't killed anyone.

He'd busted her face. His knuckles still ached from it. Smashing her head in and then her belly.

That had shut her up!

He was so turned on he couldn't hold back. He spurted in her chamber, then ran away, leaving her in a puddle of mud. Her breasts slick with rain and her tummy bruised from the beating.

Wanted to make it last all night.

Too bad.

He imagined Patsy in a ditch. Naked. Raped so hard her pussy was like a baseball glove. Her ass split, so it was like a pit filled with red clay. Her face shredded, cut, distorted. No longer beautiful. No longer innocent.

Broken.

He wanted so badly to break her open and see how warm her insides were.

Kern bit her lip. She moaned—not with pleasure, with pain—and tried to pull away from him.

He jackhammered her, driving her into his filthy, sperm-stained mattress. He pinned her down, holding her still so he could have his way with her.

By the time he was cumming, she was bleeding from her lip.

Kern tasted her blood and loved it.

He reared back, groaning as he came. Feeling his hot fluids drain out of her and cool in the wet spot below their pelvises.

He tore away from her, planted his feet on the floor, and grunted like he'd just finished lifting a concrete block.

"God, Alex," Patsy whimpered.

"Good, wasn't it?" Kern sneered, looking over his shoulder.

Patsy wasn't broken. Not the way he'd like. But she looked disheveled. Her hair was tangled, her lips were smeared in blood, and her bottom half looked wounded.

Patsy swallowed. "That . . . hurt."

"That's normal," Kern said. "It's because I'm so big."

"If you say so," Patsy said.

"I say so." Kern stood and stamped over to the bathroom. He returned with a bath towel, which he tossed at his girl.

As she cleaned herself up, Kern used a sock to sponge up his spooge.

"Well, what should we do tonight?" Patsy asked, sitting up.

"Let's go to a movie."

Patsy smiled. "Sure. That sounds nice. Which one?"

"Whatever is playing at the Metropol." He smiled, knowing that his girlfriend had no clue he would be walking her to a porno theater.

"Okay!"

And just like that, she was happy again.

Kern loved it, this game of back-and-forth. This love/hate. He wanted to make her suffer. He wanted her to think this was what love was.

This Rag
It Smells of Death

LORI WALKED HOME IN a stupefied state, holding the book to her breasts and stumbling through the crowds. She'd refused to go to the hospital after what she'd seen.

Couldn't have been real. No. No. No. Not real. A dream. You saw Bianchi have a heart attack and you freaked.

But what about what you saw earlier?

It was the same guy.

The Young Prince!

When Lori stepped into her apartment building, she barely heard Chadwick. Until he shouted her name, she almost walked past him.

Looking at him startled her.

He had bloody freckles on his face, and his knees were muddy. He looked frightened, as if he'd just lived through a war.

"Lori! Lori! You gotta hide me!"

Lori shook her head. "What?"

"No time to explain! I'll tell you soon! Please!"

Lori led him up the stairs. When they came down the hallway, she was thankful that neither Andres nor Kern were standing by their doors.

Once inside the apartment, Chadwick was whirling with panic and babbling. She couldn't make sense of any of it, so she burst out, "Bianchi died."

Chadwick paused. "What happened, girl?"

"I don't know," Lori whimpered. She used the heel of her hand to wipe away a tear. "We were talking about the book and . . . and The Young Prince burst in on us. H-he murdered Bianchi right in front of me."

Chadwick sighed. "I saw him too."

They shared their stories, this time with open ears.

"Whistler ditched me. I lay there on the ground, waiting for those things to get me. They never did. Eventually, I wandered toward yer place. Took me a while to find it."

"Oh God."

"I didn't *see* him, but I could *feel* him. It felt like a plague had broken out in the park. Like everything around me had come down with the flu. Even the grass was sickly. I don't know what happened because Whistler didn't tell me before he scampered off. But I don't blame him. I can only imagine what it was he saw."

Lori sat down and looked at the book. *The Text of the Inninian* was like a heavy cat on her lap. Organic. Thrumming. Warm.

"I don't know what's happening, Chaddy. I really don't."

"Me neither. But I think it's spelled B-A-D."

"You can say that again."

"What should we do?" Chadwick asked. "What can we do?"

"I think our answers are in this book. Only . . . we can't possibly know what it says."

"That's the real one, huh?"

"Yes. I wish we could've gotten our hands on Tanner Fishman's translation. Even if it's the ravings of a crazy person, it oughta help us figure him out."

"I don't think he's just crazy," Chadwick said.

"Neither do I. I was a skeptic this morning. Now, Tanner's made me a believer! What he did to Bianchi . . . be glad you weren't there. God. I can't even close my eyes without seeing it."

"Don't think about it. Just . . . let's decide what we're doing next."

"Yes. Good idea. I think we should call my friend, Brion, over tonight. As far as I know, he's seen nothing like we have. But he'll believe me. He knows me too well to think I've lost my marbles."

"You have his number?"

"Of course. I'll call him right away! He might still be at work, but I can leave him a message."

"Would it be okay if I take another shower?" Chadwick asked apologetically. "I got blood on me."

"Yes. Of course. I'll have Brion bring you some new clothing too. You've got blood on yours."

"I figured."

Chadwick guided himself into the bathroom. Even though the shower was running, Lori could hear him crying.

She called Brion's number.

Luckily, there was an answer.

"Hello?" a female voice asked.

"Olga?"

"Yes. This is Brion Bowyer's phone."

Lori smiled. "I'm Lori. From work."

"Oh, Brion told me about you!"

"He told me about you too. Listen, is he around?"

"No. He's at the station. But he should be back soon. He was supposed to be back already but there was something going on at the park."

Chadwick wasn't lying. Not that I figured he would.

"Yes. Well. It's about that," Lori said.

"He didn't have time to tell me what happened!" Olga said. "Was it another—"

"Yes. It was. A shooting."

Olga said something in Russian. “It’s frightening, isn’t it? Every day, a new horror!”

“I couldn’t agree more. Listen, I need to see Brion. And maybe you should come along too. Tell him when he gets home to come right over. Tell him I found something important.”

“I will. Are you okay, Lori? You weren’t at the park, were you?”

“No. I wasn’t. But I have a friend here who was. And we’ve uncovered something. Well . . . It’ll be easier to just show it to you guys. Otherwise, you’ll think I’m looney tunes. Oh, and tell Brion to bring a change of clothes with him. My friend needs them.”

Olga paused. I’ll tell him.”

“Thank you.” Lori hung up.

She stayed seated, flipping through the pages of the book while she waited for Chadwick. He came out wearing a bathrobe.

“Sorry, Lori. I think my clothes need ta be tossed. I hate to say it, but I messed myself pretty bad when that gun went off.”

“No worries.”

“You caught yer pal?”

“His girlfriend. I guess they’re moving pretty fast.” Lori smirked.

“Brion’s a good guy?”

“One of the best.”

"Good." Chadwick sat down on the loveseat. "I think we oughta keep a small circle until this thing is over. People we trust and no one else."

"I couldn't agree more." Lori looked down at the pages. She saw an illustration of a ghoul. One eye had been scooped out and looked to have been replaced by a festering ball of worms.

"Can I see it?" Chadwick asked.

"What?"

"The book."

"Oh." Lori looked down at the tome. "I mean, I don't know what it'll do for you."

"I ain't ever held a rare book before. Figure I oughta."

Lori stood and brought the book over to him. She sat it on his lap, open.

Chadwick touched the paper.

And screamed.

The Catacombs Are Their Tombs

The City Will Be Their Playground

WHISTLER RACED THROUGH THE alleys and streets, hurtling himself through debris and trash left behind by the uncaring populace. His legs slipped out from under him, and he landed on his rump next to a garbage bin. He scurried beneath it, not caring about the dumpster juice that stained his face and hands. He was sure that if he didn't stay out of sight, they would find him.

Ghouls.

Zombies.

Undead demon fucklords with hooked claws and snarling teeth.

Whatever you wanted to call 'em!

Huddled beneath the dumpster, Whistler's mind raced.

It's the end times.

Whole planet is gonna get fucked-up and run over by those . . . things!

No one will be spared!

Oh God. Chadwick!

Now that he had time to reflect, he realized what a shitty thing it'd been to leave Chadwick behind. The poor old geezer didn't deserve to get torn up. Hell, no one did! Whistler wondered if he oughta just kill himself and get it over with, atone for his sins. He felt like shit.

Looking around at the scraps and clumps of fecal-smelling fungi beneath the dumpster, he decided he belonged down here.

I deserve worse than death.

Oh, Chadwick. I'm so sorry. I wish I could go back and change things. I'm a coward. A stupid coward. Just left you high and dry. You couldn't even see what was comin' ta getcha!

Crying, Whistler checked to make sure the coast was clear. No one was pursuing him. He'd made it. He'd survived.

At the cost of his conscience.

He dragged himself out from beneath the dumpster. Egg-yolk-thick patches of scum decorated his front and knotted his hair. Whistler wiped his face, then stumbled down the alley. He had no clue where he was or where he was going. He just hoped he'd find a rambling train around the next corner. He'd hop on it and ride outta town like he'd never lived here to begin with.

Whistler came around the corner and found himself on a derelict street. The pavement was untended, and the shops looked deserted. He came upon an apartment building and was surprised to note that every single window had been knocked out. Shards of shattered glass littered the asphalt.

What is this place?

The city has some bad spots . . . but it ain't got no ghost towns!

Swallowing a lump, Whistler looked around, hoping to spot some sign of normalcy. A woman pushing a stroller. An old man reading on a bench. A group of kids playing cops and robbers near the road. A passing car. ANYTHING!

The air felt weird. The way it had when he'd seen The Young Prince.

He decided it was time to leave.

Something groaned ahead of him.

Whistler froze.

Two corpses were shambling in his direction. They'd appeared out of thin air. A male with puffy boils, and a woman whose face was half-melted tar. The man's belly was open, and his organs hung out like a clump of severed dog tongues. The woman was nude. Everything aside from her face was beautiful.

No!

How'd they find me?

A thick curtain of fog bellowed out from the manhole covers and the sewer grates. The white haze engulfed Whistler's surroundings, making him feel as if he'd somehow stepped *inside* a static channel on the television.

Snowy fists knocked him backward. His mouth moved in a screwy pattern, producing no sound but accumulating frightened moisture.

The zombies groaned.

"Whistler . . . Whistler . . . Come here!"

Whistler spun around, hoping to run.

There were more zombies! They had him from all sides! The ones behind him were both children. One was a boy whose skull had been caved in. He was wearing school clothes, and his lips had peeled away, exposing a line of yellowed chompers.

Next to him was a zombie that could have been his sister. A six-year-old with pale skin, sunken eyes, and bloodstained cheeks. Her hair was in pigtails, and she was wearing a pleated skirt.

"Help!" Whistler screamed.

No windows popped open. No townspeople rushed out to rescue the distressed man.

"Help!"

The children mocked him. They repeated his calls in a snide, cruel, belligerent tone, "Help! Help!"

They were closing in on him.

Whistler peeled away from them, rushing onto the road.

The fog grew thicker, blinding him.

If any cars go through this . . .

They won't see me until it's too late!

Panting, Whistler rushed across the street and found himself on the other side. He was relieved he hadn't been struck by a passing motorist, but he was also dismayed that there'd been no passing motorists! He felt utterly alone.

Just me . . . and the zombies!

He realized that this street was similarly populated with the undead. They shambled toward him, moving slowly despite their hungry eyes and salivating mouths.

The nearest one was wearing a hospital frock. Half of his brain was exposed.

Behind him stood a tall woman with blue bruises and an open shirt. Her breasts had been bitten so much they looked like hunks of butchered meat from a shop window. Her white pants were stained red with gore.

Whistler turned back and forth, trying to find a spot to run to. Seeking safety.

A girl leapt at him from out of the fog. She raked her nails across his screaming face, digging deep trenches in his cheeks.

Whistler screamed and jumped away, feeling his face and the running blood with his fuzzy mittens.

His heels buffered the edge of a stone staircase. Without hesitating, he spun around, grabbed the handrail, and dashed up.

"Whistler! Help! Help, Whistler! Help!" the zombies crowed. They started to amass around the bottom of the steps, but none dared move up them. Whistler was too panicked to notice their immobility. To him, they were right behind him. Scratching his skin and grabbing his hair and—

He banged against the door like he was a battering ram. The door swung open. Whistler tumbled into the building.

Weeping, he scrambled to his feet and slammed the door shut behind him, holding it closed and praying to God that the undead would give up and leave him be.

From outside, he could hear the wind blowing through the fog. He could hear the zombies hissing his name. Moaning it. Almost orgasmic.

Whistler rested his brow against the door and prayed again.

"Our Father, Who art in Heaven, hallowed be Thy name—"

"Whistler! Come out! Whistler!" the zombies moaned.

Whistler stepped away from the door and crossed himself.

"In Jesus's name, I revoke you!"

The zombies all laughed.

Whistler held his hands over his mouth and continued praying. In his mind, if he stopped praying, then God would abandon him. He'd be like bait dropped into a shark-infested sea. They'd come crashing through the door, and they'd surround him, and they'd *eat him*. Just like that bald lady who'd chewed on her victims.

Did they answer her prayers? Did they make her one of their soldiers? By killing her?

Whistler cupped his hand over his seeping cheek. The blood was hot and slimy.

He prayed to himself as he took in his surroundings. Streams of fog leaked through the broken windows and swirled around him, blurring his vision. He knew he was in the hollowed husk of a building, but he could not tell what the building had been before it'd been scooped clean. A few chairs sat sporadically around him. Wicker chairs with torn undersides and tilted legs. One was even backless.

He noticed a painting on the farthest wall. It was crude and dark. Colorless. It portrayed a naked woman and naked man looking up toward a giant eyeball, which was projecting warm rays of wavering sunlight. Their faces were distorted. It seemed to be on purpose, not due to the artist's inexperience.

"What is this place?" Whistler asked aloud. "Where am I?"

"HELL!" a gristly voice croaked behind him.

Whistler spun around.

A length of clacking rusty chain swept toward him like a scorpion's stinger. It struck his face, slicing his cheek and tearing it open. More blood spouted from the wound and spritzed the floor. Holding his face, Whistler stumbled back, crying out with agony and panic.

"HELL!" the demonic voice roared again before swiping the chain back toward Whistler. It struck him on the scalp, tearing open the seam between hair and forehead. Blood fountained from the hole and oozed down Whistler's gasping face, tinting his vision crimson before outright blinding him.

He couldn't see his assailant, but he could hear the creature—there was no way it was human—laughing. It struck again and again. The chain felt like a metallic fist, pummeling his gut and then his shoulder. His fur coat muffled the blows somewhat. These two knocks drew no blood, but they did disorient him.

Whistler tried to run, but he became tangled in one of the stray chairs. Yipping, he tumbled and smashed his face onto the dirty, fog-coated floor.

The chain dug into his back, like a curious finger drawing a trench through a sandbox. Blood funneled up into the air, streaming jubilantly from his quaking body.

"God is my protector!" Whistler shouted, army crawling ahead and dragging his legs behind him. "He protects me!"

"Your God is *filth*!" the attacker hissed.

The chains clinked and clanged, then whipped down toward Whistler. He squalled when they found his buttocks, lashing them.

Whistler cried out. His rotten teeth grinding together. His gums and jaws burned, as if they'd been injected with hot wax.

Whistler felt hands around him. More zombies.

They hefted him up and brought him to the wall, pinning him to it. He turned his head and blinked until he could see.

The painting was beside him.

Two inhuman worshipers and their nebulous god.

The undead that surrounded him were like carnival figures. Wax models created to incite horror and repulsion alone. One was a woman with moldy teeth and snotty bubbles coating her dour face. Another was a man with half of his face peeled away and the other half swollen with bruises.

The chain-swinging ghoul stood a ways away, holding his clinking chains and smiling at Whistler. He was only wearing a plastic crown, and his chest had been hollowed out. He looked like a walking honeycomb.

"Please, have mercy!" Whistler panted.

"God showed no mercy. Why should *we*?" Chains cackled.

Whistler looked from zombie to zombie, hoping one of them had at least a sliver of a soul left in their rotted husks. Praying that one would loosen their grip on his outstretched arms.

They're holding me prone. Like I'm going to be crucified.

Chains walked toward him, swinging his weapon like a pinwheel.

The gray metal sang to Whistler.

Whistler screamed in response.

The metal struck. It drew the flesh away from Whistler's face, revealing patches of wilted, tender, rusty muscle. He shook in place, tugging at the zombies who restrained him.

His efforts were worthless.

Chains hit the homeless man again.

Whistler felt his eye pop in its socket, struck by the metallic weapon. It sank, then deflated, discharging its contents down his glittery cheek.

"Grovel! Grovel and weep!" Chains demanded.

"God!" Whistler gulped. His mouth was filled with blood. His right eye had blurred with tears. His ears were ringing. His skin felt as if it had been lit aflame.

"Pray to the Inninian!"

"No! I won't!" Whistler brayed.

The chains snapped on his stomach. He doubled over, twisting his arms.

"Lift his shirts!" Chains snarled.

The zombies went to work, peeling Whistler's clothing away from him. He felt naked without his fur coat. When his shirt was rucked up, exposing his distended, bruised belly, he felt as if he'd been molested.

"I won't!" Whistler stated. "I won't worship your false god!"

"Blasphemer!" Chains hissed.

"I won't!"

The chains dropped to the ground, coiling like a metal snake.

The zombie stepped toward the victim. His tongue crept out of his foul mouth and licked his black teeth.

"First you will quiver. Then you will scream. Then, child, you will die!"

Whistler clenched his fists. He spat.

The zombie reached into his own rib cage. He dug around. Whistler could hear the ghoul's talon-sharp nails scraping its bones and dehydrated gristle.

When he pulled his hand out, he was holding a new weapon. A spike with an oak handle and a long rod at its center that sat between the creature's middle and ring fingers. The rod was about eight inches long and ended with a needle-sharp point.

It twinkled in the strange lighting.

"Quiver!" The zombie punched Whistler in the belly. The pain was instant and stinging, as if Whistler had been attacked by the world's largest hornet.

The zombie extracted the spike. It gleamed with black blood. Whistler could hear air and liquid escaping from the wound. He'd been stabbed right above his chestnut-sized navel.

"Scream!" The zombie sank the spike into the spot just beneath Whistler's sternum. He could feel the metal sliding against the bone. It was as if someone was scratching his own tombstone with rusty nails.

He couldn't help it.

Whistler began to scream.

He yowled as if he truly believed someone would hear him . . . come to him . . . SAVE HIM!

"Die!" the zombie roared.

Chains plunged the spike into Whistler's remaining eyeball. It popped instantly before the weapon descended into Whistler's skull, then exited through the back of his cranium. The bones crunched, and the speared brain sparked in a last-ditch effort to save Whistler's life.

The zombie yanked the spike free. Blood oozed out Whistler's eye socket and sprayed from the back of his skull, painting the wall behind him a bright and angry shade of scarlet.

The zombies released Whistler and watched him slump to the floor.

Without a word, the fiends left his body. They shambled out of the building and searched for their next victims.

That was the beautiful thing about the city.

There was always fresh meat around every corner.

I Hate What I Must See

Lori yanked the book away from Chadwick, startled by his shouting. He stopped instantly, blinking his blind eyes and working his loose mouth.

"What happened?" Lori asked.

"I saw *Hell*!"

"What do you mean?"

"I touched the book . . . and I saw where it had been written! Not Earth! No. Down in the deepest bowels of Hell. Oh, Lori! It's terrible! It's worse than we thought!"

Chadwick began to weep.

Lori hesitated. "Are you . . . psychic?"

"No. Never before. I haven't even heard the voice of God, although I pray to him nightly." Chadwick clutched himself. "This was different. It wasn't a vision. It was as if I'd been transported from here . . . to there!"

"Where?"

"Into the depths. Into the pits. Into the heart of the inferno. Into the home of that dreadful family." Chadwick's eyes brimmed with red tears.

"Oh God! You're bleeding!" Lori shouted.

"I saw the Inninian, Lori. I saw them!"

Lori rushed into the kitchen. She returned with a towel and delicately dabbed away the bloody tears that streaked Chadwick's wrinkled, hairy cheeks.

"I keep closing my eyes and expecting to wake up from this nightmare," Lori said.

"It won't happen. It will only get worse. My God. You can't imagine it, Lori. And you'll go mad if you see it. No wonder Tanner turned out the way he did. Communicating with them . . . even just hearing their breathing! It's enough to break the mind and soul."

"What are they?" Lori asked.

"Demons. Gods. Something else. I don't know. But they exist. They live in Hell. And they're here. Two of them are in our city!"

"The Foul Twins," Lori said.

"Yes! And I know their names!" Chadwick coughed. "Barsipher-Maagrer-Et-Inninian and Ill-Et-Ellion-Inninian. The Young Prince and The Unholy Whore!"

Lori's windows exploded.

Glass sprinkled the floor, followed by violent, punching gusts of putrid-scented wind. It felt as if an entire dumpster of hospital sick had been poured into Lori's apartment.

Lori hugged the book close to her chest with one arm and stifled her nose with the other. Coughing violently, she and Chadwick got to their feet and backed away from the yawning windows.

The wind was shrieking, deafening, banshee-like in its incessancy.

"Lori!" Chadwick moaned, then retched. She watched him hurl a thread of bile, doubling up and clutching his stomach. "What is that smell?"

"It's death!" Lori moaned. "Oh God! It's *death*!"

Her curtains blew apart. Lori saw shifting yellow eyes staring into her apartment, piercing and lewd. The eyes of perverts and murderers.

"We need to go!" Chadwick said.

"No!" Lori said. "We can't leave! It's dangerous out there!"

The wind picked up, blasting Lori's cheeks and face. She felt as if she was being rubbed raw with sandpaper and struck with wet slaps. The smell was crawling into her pores, infecting her body. She wanted to be away from it, but she was also aware that it was purposefully driving her and Chadwick to her door.

What if we go into the hall . . . and run into something worse? We can't risk it!

"The Inninian can raise the dead, Lori!" Chadwick shouted. "I saw it in Hell. They are served by living corpses!"

"We can't leave!" Lori repeated, hating the taste that assaulted her tongue whenever she opened her mouth.

"The city will be crawling with the undead! They will have an army in hours! It's already too late. We have to leave!" Chadwick shouted. "Please, Lori!"

"No, Chadwick! We have to stop them!" She gritted her teeth together and pulled the book closer to her chest. It felt as if the leather-bound tome was squirming in her grip. Like an oversized pill bug.

"Hell! They want to make Hell on Earth!"

The wind stopped.

The lights flickered, then faded.

In the darkness, Lori gasped for breath. The disgusting stench dissipated, much to her relief. Like sewage slipping down an opened pipe.

The lights came back on.

Lori gasped.

They were no longer alone in her apartment.

"What is it, Lori?" Chadwick shouted.

"Be quiet!" she whispered.

Lori stepped back until she was standing next to her blind friend. She linked her arm through his and tugged him near.

Chadwick groaned. “It’s the same scent from the park. Like hot blood and the flu—”

“Shush!” Lori commanded.

The three zombies all turned toward her, as if they’d been pulled in by her noise. They stood in place, wavering on their crinkling legs.

The zombies were all petrified. Their skin had shrunk against their skeletons. Their heads were rumpled, as if their brains had curdled in their skulls. Their teeth grew past their lips, more like hog tusks than human chompers.

One wore a burlap sack. Another wore a robe. The third was naked. His shriveled prick looked like a dead mole sitting on a dirty mound.

“I can hear them!” Chadwick whispered.

“Be quiet!” Lori snapped.

The zombies all cocked their heads in unison, drawn to their noises.

“It’s the undead,” Lori quietly explained. “They’re with us. We must be silent.”

Understanding, Chadwick sealed his lips.

The nude zombie took a jarring step toward them, lifting up his spindly, rakish arms. His fingers looked like prongs.

“Fucking shit!” Lori cried.

“What is it?” Chadwick asked.

The zombie moaned. It was a low, guttural, animalistic noise. It brought to mind a starved and mangy tiger.

Someone knocked at the door behind them.

"Hey! What's with all the noise?" Andres hollered. "We're tryin' ta shoot a movie over here!"

Please, Andres! Please, please, please, shut the fuck up!

The zombie lurched ahead.

Lori shoved Chadwick to the side, stepping out of the zombie's way just in time.

She heard the doorknob joggle. Andres was furious.

"Whatever you're doing in there, it's too damn loud! Breaking glass and shit! C'mon, bitch! This isn't a slum!"

The zombie crashed into the door. His arms burst through it and out the other side, splintering wood with successive pops and cracks!

Andres screeched, but the zombie had him by the hair. He heaved back, dragging Andres's head through the fractured center of the door. It looked as if he was forcing his own head into Lori's apartment.

He braced himself against the door frame, trying and failing to worm his way out of the ghoul's grip. His mouth—open and screaming—was raked across the edge of the broken wood. Lori saw sharp splinters of wood spear and tear his lips, shredding them like paper. The wood gritted against his clenched teeth.

Andres twisted and turned, groaning weakly as his mouth bled onto the carpet below.

The zombie forced his head down. Now the splinters of wood were piercing his neck. Poking the flesh before they broke through.

Blood spilled out of Andres in rapid currents and spurting waves.

"Fucker!' Andres groaned. "I'll fuckin' kill you!"

The zombie slammed down on Andres's skull, sinking the fractured wood through his throat. It prodded the flesh on the scruff of his neck, then split it. Red blood spewed from the entrance and exit points. Andres gurgled and cried, mewling like a distempered infant.

He fell limp suddenly. Red bubbles burst from his tattered lips.

That's the second death I've witnessed today.

Let's see them call that *a heart attack!*

Lori and Chadwick backed away until their rumps hit one of Lori's overstocked bookshelves.

The other zombies remained where they stood, like fetid mannequins.

The nude ghoul ripped Andres's head away from his body with a grunting pull. They heard his torso hit the ground outside of Lori's apartment.

Holding the bleeding, mutilated head, the naked zombie turned toward Lori and Chadwick.

"First . . . we're going to kill you!" he enunciated in a clear voice. "Then . . . we're going to eat you!"

A hole punched through the zombie's chest, followed by an expulsion of inky fluid.

The zombie stumbled, dropping Andres's head. The skull shattered upon hitting the ground, like a rotten pumpkin dropped from a balcony. Snotty tissue issued from the fissures in his cranium and stained the already-ruined carpet.

The zombie turned, snarling angrily.

The door swung open.

Kern stepped in, holding his six-shooter. The well-oiled gun looked tiny in his massive paw.

His lip curled into a sinister smirk.

He fired again at close range. This time through the zombie's throat.

"Kern!" Lori shouted.

Ignoring her, he watched as the zombie stepped back, then charged him.

He set the muzzle of the gun between the zombie's eyes and yanked the trigger. This bullet kicked the back of the skull wide open. The zombie released a sizzling noise before he crumpled to the floor.

Lori pulled Chadwick over, finding shelter behind their giant savior.

Kern looked at the other corpses. They walked toward him, arms raised and mouths yawning wide.

"Take that, you son of a bitch!" He fired into the zombie wearing the burlap sack. The zombie jumped as a hole was knocked into his belly. After a wobbly moment, he continued to approach them.

Kern fired again. This bullet hit the creature in his heart. It caused the zombie to seize up, as if he'd been shocked. In seconds, he seemed to recover from the wound and continue his pursuit.

Kern reset his aim and fired directly into the zombie's skull. The head shattered as if it'd been struck with an aluminum bat.

The body thumped to the ground like a puppet whose strings had been severed.

The final zombie—wearing a robe—was near enough to grab at Kern's arm. He knocked his elbow into its face, discombobulating it.

Kern quickly popped the cylinder open and emptied the spent shells onto Lori's carpet. He reached into the pocket of his tight jeans, extracted more bullets, and loaded the rounds one at a time.

"Thank God you heard us!" Lori shouted.

"Don't thank me yet. The whole city is overrun. My girl and I were about to leave when I looked out the window!" Kern stated.

He lifted his gun and fired into the nearby zombie. The sound of the gunshot was like a god clapping his hands. A patch of the robe split, and Lori saw the zombie's deflated breast pop. Kern was quick to drop the hammer and fire again, planting another bullet into the ghoul's gut.

"The head!" Lori screeched. "Shoot it in the head!"

Kern raised the gun. This shot popped the zombie's nose in. Blood squirted from the cavernous wound. The zombie cried and groaned, then tipped backward, hitting its head on Lori's coffee table and shattering it.

"C'mon!" Kern swept around, grabbing Lori's hand and dragging her across the hall. She pulled Chadwick after her.

She tried not to look at Andres's body, but it was impossible not to.

The headless corpse was being towed down the hallway by a fat zombie, who was already munching through Andres's Achilles tendon.

Kern paused long enough to put a bullet into the zombie's head, then he, Lori, and Chadwick went into his apartment and shut the door.

Amok City

OUTSIDE, DAY TURNED TO night all too soon. It was only just the evening when the sun died and was replaced by a thick, membranous black cloak. One that swirled over the city, shielding it from the rest of the world and from the eyes of Heaven.

Darkness fell.

The second it did . . . the dead rose.

Porn

0

Manners was sitting in his favorite porno theater. The Millcreek Metropol was discreet, classy, and never targeted by the cops. The patrons were often wealthy and never wanted to be outed. Secrecy was a way of life here, especially considering the films they whacked off to.

Manners was watching one right now. On the screen, a woman was being tied to a rusty bed. The mattress was stained with the blood of the previous victim. She'd been ugly. This one . . . she was perfect.

Keaton Manners—the face of the morning news and a trustworthy member of society—licked his lips.

No one at work knew he was a snuff film addict, and he was happy to keep it that way. But he'd rather be caught than give it up. Especially when, lately, the filmmakers had stepped things up a notch.

They knew the overseas market had raised the bar, and so these American entrepreneurs had to become more innovative. New ways to torture, mutilate, and kill. Younger, prettier victims. Kinkier exploits. No longer was it accepted that they could just roll a camera and cut a throat. Not with an audience that was frothing at the mouth for more depravity and hedonism.

No. They had to get creative.

In the dark theater, Manners undid his belt and unzipped his fly. His penis rose from his pants like a corpse from a coffin. Without hesitating, he spat on his left palm and began to wax his rod. His grip was tight, and his breathing was heavy.

There were a few other people around him. He could hear them squeezing their meat as well. All of them wore trench coats and fedora hats, hiding their identities as best they could.

I could be schmoozing with the elite here, and I wouldn't know it!

Manners showed his teeth and worked his crank. He liked pulling down hard enough to tauten the skin. He had once masturbated so hard he came blood. That'd been one hell of a good nut!

The girl on screen was perfect.

She was mentally disabled.

When they'd brought her into the bloodstained kill room, she'd been hugging a teddy and rocking on her heels, wearing a helmet on her fuzzy head. She couldn't have been older than eighteen, but she had the mind of a trusting child.

She spoke to her captors—two oily, muscled men wearing dog masks—and Manners was thankful this film had audio.

"Y-you said you'd take me home!"

They were gonna do that all right. Take her all the way home!

They'd stripped her roughly, tearing her teddy out of her hands and ripping it apart in front of her weeping face. Those cries had gotten Manners so stiff, he was pretty sure he was in danger of breaking a blood vessel.

They dragged her to the bed. Naked and kicking, she gave the camera a full view of her untrimmed pussy and her pale, doughy flesh.

They laid her down on the bed, wrapping her head with so many leather belts she looked like an ancient mummy. Then they took turns raping her.

After that, they started in with the belt sander.

Someone sat beside Manners.

He turned his head and was shocked to see a woman next to him.

He wondered if he oughta put his business back in its drawer.

The girl was screaming again, though, and Manners was so close.

He looked back at the screen and grinned at the crimson images.

"Are you having fun?" the woman asked.

Seething, he turned toward her.

She was pretty. Blonde and curvy. Looked like a whore he'd once banged during his birthday party.

"What's it to you?" he asked. "You a cop or something?"

Softly, the woman chuckled. "No. No, I'm not."

To his surprise, one of her hands climbed up her front like a spider. It latched onto her clothed breast and began to rub.

Smiling, Manners continued to pump his pork sword. He flashed a happy and mischievous grin at her.

Her other hand crept onto his lap. It whisked up his thigh, then encircled his throbbing prick.

Shit. Am I about to get a handy?

Manners, overjoyed, looked from the screen to the mysterious woman sitting beside him. She was smiling as well, showing each and every tooth in her mouth.

They were sharp.

Canine like.

He rotated his hips, helping fill her palm with his angry cock. It was burning and pulsing, eager to cum but worried about blasting off before things got really good.

His resistance was rewarded.

She leaned over, slumped down, then vacuumed his organ into her moist maw. She scraped her teeth against the underside of his rod, not unpleasantly, and teased his winking slit with the tip of her nimble tongue.

"Oh, baby!" Manners exclaimed, pumping his hips so he could tickle the back of her throat. She didn't gag or *hrrrrk*.

"Good girl!" He stroked the back of her head, running his fingers through her golden hair.

Just as he began to spurt . . . the zombie bit.

Her teeth seared through his thin flesh and hardened tissue. He could feel spongy matter unspool from the stub of his castrated cock, painting her chomping, salivating lips.

Manners opened his mouth to scream.

His mouth was instantly filled with fingers.

He writhed in place, crying and groaning before the zombie yanked his jaw away from his face with one savage pull. Blood sprayed and spewed from his exposed oral cavity.

Manners clawed at the gushing wound, crying as he died.

No one else in the theater seemed to notice. They were too entranced by the sordid visuals ahead of them and the pleasures in their calloused palms.

The zombie stood, shuffled down the rows, and chose her next victim.

Punks on Junk

"WHAT'S THE MATTER WITH you?" Applegate screamed, throwing his middle finger up and pumping his dirty fist. He was so sick of this city. Sick of being pushed around by crowds, sick of working in a goddamned filthy bodega, and sick of jerk-ass cabbies driving right past him even when he was half off the curb. He was especially sick of puddles and of being splashed.

Maybe I oughta move to the country. Momma said the city was no place for me. Sure, Mom. Whatever you say, Mom.

Fuck.

Momma was right!

Applegate used the front of his shirt to clean his grime-pebbled face. The water that crashed into him was stagnant and filmy. It was the pollution, he knew. It clung to everything and everyone.

Those nutjobs have the right idea. Going postal seems like the natural solution to all this madness.

Phil Applegate sighed heavily. Of course he wasn't a*ctually* going to go nuts and take a machine gun to a shopping mall. He wasn't the type. Even when he was angry, the worst result was a burst blood vessel and a bitten tongue. He couldn't afford to go nuts the way this wave of recent crazies had.

But sometimes, only to himself, he liked to fantasize about it. Liked to imagine lobbing a grenade underneath a car that'd just hit a puddle at full speed and doused him in gutter slime. He also pictured storming into a high school and taking out as many kids as he could, because teenagers truly made his life a living hell at the bodega. They shoplifted, ate from the aisles, and harassed him. Sometimes they even robbed from the plastic tip jar that sat by his register! And when inventory was low, Applegate's boss was quick to blame his employees rather than the snot-nosed brats who stormed into the bodega and overwhelmed it after school let out.

Fuckers.

Patting his front, Phil Applegate stormed down the street, muttering tersely through tight teeth. His vision was blurred with anger and depression. His hands were clenched into fists.

Applegate was a slovenly dude. His hair was greasy and curly. His nose was blistered, and his skin was so dry his cheeks were always flaking. His high school acne had left deep black pits all over his face. He was also tall.

Some folks called him "The Ogre."

One brazen teen had even told him he had a face cut out for crime.

He wished.

This country seemed to reward criminals more than decent, mild-mannered, hardworking citizens like Applegate.

Lotta good the high road did me.

Applegate looked toward the sky. It was pitch-black. Unusual, but he wasn't bothered by it. Anymore, it seemed like night snuck up early and goosed the city into a semi-panic. Well, Applegate was going to be the master of his own feelings. He wasn't going to be scared of the dark.

He walked down the street, ignoring the roiling fog and the lack of people. He was thankful not to be trapped in the middle of a stampeding herd of inconsiderate citizens for once.

Smacking his lips and pocketing his hands, he tried to think of how relieving it would be to get home. He'd shuck off his clothes, take a relaxing shower, then sit in front of the tube and chug enough beer to give him a dreamless night.

He hated dreaming. Hated being forced to endure as much ridiculousness in his sleep as he did in the waking world.

"Hey!"

He turned his head.

A group of punks were coming up behind him.

Bracing himself, as if he was preparing to run into a wall, Applegate turned and kept walking. He'd only gotten a brief look at the kids, but it was enough to confirm they weren't the sort to run up and ask for directions.

There'd been a fat one with bleached hair and a nose ring. A slender skinhead with an Army jacket. A girl with half her head shaved and the other side braided. She wore a swastika patch on her arm.

They'll probably jump me. It's happened before.

I just wanna go home.

"Hey!" one of the boys shouted. He guessed it was the skinny one.

Let 'em try. Just let 'em try it with me. They'll see I'm not the one to fuck with. Goddamn stupid junkie punk mofos!

Applegate rotated his fingers around the switchblade he kept in his pocket. The illegal knife had been stolen from a teen customer who'd left his bookbag on the counter while he shoplifted from the bodega.

You take something of mine, I'll swipe somethin' of yours! he'd thought while plucking the weapon from the bag.

He felt safer with the blade, but he'd never had cause to use it since procuring it. It was as if owning a weapon put a cloud around him that told the city's weirdos to BACK THE FUCK OFF!

Except these three punks. They were too dumb and headstrong to see the blaring red warning signs over Applegate's head.

The skinny kid grabbed Applegate's shoulder.

He spun around, flicking the blade out in a fluid, practiced motion. The knife seemed to smile as it sliced through the air and slashed the punk's throat.

"Oh, shit!" the fat one hollered.

"Jones!" the girl cried.

Applegate stepped back, watching the results of his work. The skinhead, Jones, fumbled around, gasping as blood spilled down his front and filled his gray mouth.

Jones hit the street, falling down like a stiff board. He didn't shake or seize the way Applegate expected. Instead, he blew red bubbles, whimpered, then expired with a harsh rattle.

Dead.

The gravity of what he'd done struck him like a pineapple-sized fist.

But he couldn't be blamed. The cops would see it his way. This worthless junked-up punk had grabbed him, after all. Out of nowhere.

I have the right to protect myself, Applegate thought.

He looked up at the remaining punks. They were mortified.

"Y-you killed him!" the girl whined. "We weren't gonna hurt you!"

"Stay back!" Applegate shouted, even though no one was approaching him.

"We were . . . we were gonna warn you!" the girl cried.

Warn me? About what?

The white-haired kid knelt down and touched his friend's wrist. "He's dead. He's dead and you killed him!"

"I'll do the same to the rest of ya if you come at me like yer pal did!" Applegate said.

The boy stood and rushed to the girl's side. Holding her, they backed away.

"I hope they get you!" the girl screeched. "I hope they get you and tear you to pieces! You *shit*!"

He didn't know what she meant by that.

In moments, the two had disappeared into the fog.

Applegate looked at his prize. The dead punk had bled into the gutter. The back of his pants looked doughy.

No one seemed to be coming out to investigate the commotion.

And why would they? It ain't like I killed someone that mattered.

Just another rat in the nest.

Fucker.

Deserved what he got.

If I hadn't acted, who knows what they'd have done to me! They could've robbed me and killed me. Maybe even raped me just for shits and giggles! I had no other choice but to act, and I got nuthin' to feel bad about.

Applegate heard a low and muffled groan.

Was the boy still alive?

No.

The other one had checked his pulse.

So? He wasn't a doctor.

Just as Applegate was about to hunch down and search for a pulse, he heard the groan again.

It wasn't coming from the teenager.

It was coming from behind him.

Applegate turned, holding his knife up and preparing for another scrap. He licked his lips and blinked his heavy lids rapidly.

"C'mon. Come an' get a piece of me!" Applegate shouted.

The zombie broke through the fog.

Its appearance astounded Applegate. He'd never seen anything like it before.

The creature was waterlogged and bloated. It had a pregnant belly, pendulous breasts, and only half of a head. It held its hands ahead of it. Each finger was an overgrown corkscrew.

Applegate felt his breath freeze in his mouth. His eyes widened and his bladder collapsed, spilling warm liquid down his trembling thighs.

The zombie opened what remained of its mouth. Frayed lips, cracked and crumbling teeth, fifty percent of the tongue, and a deflated, yawning gullet.

It ain't a trick. No person could walk around like that, with only half a head!

But this was impossible.

Applegate didn't believe in zombies; therefore, they couldn't exist.

Yet here one was. Blundering toward him on slow feet, groaning through its dissected maw.

"N-no!" Applegate said.

The zombie moaned and swiped at him. He responded, swinging his knife to meet her clawed hands. He watched as her fingers slid away and plopped onto the ground, writhing like fat maggots.

The zombie howled and pulled its mutilated hand back.

Emboldened, Applegate speared her pregnant belly with his blade.

A fetid odor assaulted his nose.

He pulled the knife back, looking down at it in horror. Extracting the knife, he'd brought out some of her internal contents. The blade was coated in spaghetti strand worms, wriggling centipedes, and even some hissing roaches.

He looked at the gash he'd left in her. Sloppy gruel leaked from the hole and trickled down her bare leg. The liquid was chunky and gray, like expired porridge. It smelled, too, like nothing he'd ever smelled before. As if his nose had been plugged up the sphincter of a sun-dried elephant corpse.

He tipped the switchblade. The worms and roaches slid off and spattered onto the ground. Some scurried away. Others writhed in place.

Grunting, the zombie stepped away, tending to her broken hands. Snuffling like a child who'd lost her favorite toy. Tears leaked from her remaining eye and glimmered on her singular cheek.

Applegate found himself apologizing.

"I-I'm sorry."

The zombie cried pitifully, then stepped back into the fog. Vanishing like a figment of his imagination.

Applegate didn't know what to do. He stood on the street and shivered from head to toe, wondering how he'd wake up in the morning after a night like—

A pair of strong arms wrapped around him.

Applegate screamed as he was tussled back and forth. He tightened his fist around his weapon, not wanting to lose it in the midst of this attack.

He tilted his head so he could see his attacker.

It was the punk.

The dead punk.

The one *he'd* killed.

Applegate knocked his skull back, trying to dislodge the fiend.

The zombified punk bit into the side of Applegate's head, mulching his ear and spraying blood. It ripped away the flesh in an all too easy pull, then began to loudly chew.

Applegate shrieked.

He slammed his knife over his shoulder and into the face of his assailant. He could hear the blade crunching through the zombie's cheekbone.

The creature let him go.

Applegate spilled onto the ground, spinning so he was on his rump, looking up at the zombie that had peeled the side of his face wide open.

The punk grabbed the switchblade by its handle and tugged it out of his face. Blood jettisoned from the hole in a creamy wave. Scraps of tissue hung from the zombie's slow-moving, chewing mouth.

Can't be real.

Can't be happening.

Can't be.

Applegate stood and ran, leaving the zombie behind.

He broke through the mist, only to squeal to a stop.

The fog was full of them.

The walking dead lumbered toward him.

They all looked like dark silhouettes, but he could smell them. He could hear their mummified groans and childlike cries.

The girl's words came to him again.

I hope they get you and tear you to pieces.

In a matter of seconds . . . they did just that.

There Is No Sun in the Chambers of the Dead

Jon Kirkus walked with Rachel Lovitz, holding her close. He knew she'd loved Jones, even though Timmy Jones wasn't the sort of guy who settled for one babe. But even unrequited love was love. It counted. And losing Jones—especially in such a stupid manner—must have felt like a knife to her heart,

Selfishly, Jon enjoyed the attention. Rachel had set her crying face against his shoulder, wetting and snotting up the fabric of his shirt.

I'll never clean this shirt.

Jon swallowed a lump. He didn't know what was happening to their city. All he knew was one second, they'd been smoking in an alley, and the next, they'd been running for their lives when a stream of corpses pushed their way up to the surface from a manhole, just as the sun blinked out and darkness descended on them all.

Zombies. Honest-to-God zombies. Never thought this would happen to me!

Jon held Rachel against him as they turned a corner, finding themselves in another wasteland of a street.

A car had jumped the curb and seemed to have high centered atop a fire hydrant. Water gushed from beneath the car like blood from the body of a slain animal.

Half of a corpse hung out the front of the car. It looked like a man, but the body was too flayed to truly tell.

On the street, a body lay. It had been scooped open and a trail of innards stretched between its splayed legs. Again, Jon couldn't tell what sex the body was, only that it was dead.

"I'm scared, Jon," Rachel admitted.

He nodded, agreeing with her. It was the first time he'd ever seen Rachel so vulnerable. Usually, she was tougher than dirt. He'd even once seen her start and win a bar fight with two dudes that were twice her size.

Jon, Jones, and Rachel had been drawn together by their mutual philosophy of white supremacy. Now, all of that felt like bullshit. The end of the world had put their wasted time into perspective.

Still, he wanted her. Jon was a virgin, and he didn't want to die without getting some.

Maybe I can lead her into one of these buildings. And if she says no, well . . . who's gonna stop me?

No. Even for him, it was a cruel thought. It brought to mind the recent string of violent sexual assaults that had taken place at the city park. The crimes perpetrated by someone nicknamed Baghead.

He'd be no better than that creep if he—

But who'd stop him? Really?

"Maybe we should find shelter," Jon found himself suggesting.

"Yeah. Good idea."

He looked across the street and toward an apartment building. "Come on. Let's go in here!"

Together, they rushed to the building and raced up its steps. The door swung open, and they were relieved to find a zombie-free lobby.

Jon shut the door behind them.

"Where'd that fog come from?" Rachel asked.

"The fog was the least of my concerns," Jon said. "Were those really . . . the undead?"

"I think so. Some of them looked like they shouldn't have even been standing. I'm terrified," Rachel mewled. "I've never been so scared in all my life."

Jon bit his lower lip. He loved the way her body felt against his. Firm in some spots, squishy in others. He was practically salivating, wishing he could tear her clothes off and put it to her.

How can you even think *about sex at a time like this?* Jon thought. *The city is literally being eaten alive, and you're thinking with your dick!*

Jon shuddered. He felt like an idiot and a scoundrel, but it was all he could think about—sticking his sword into Rachel's warm, moist, slick chamber.

He'd imagined her pussy before. Imagined it hairy, imagined it bald, and always imagined it dripping wet. Glinting open like a hungry mouth between her strong legs.

He was glad Jones was dead. Glad there was no competition left. As far as they knew, Jon was the last man on Earth, and Rachel was the last woman.

He tightened his arms around her, snuggling her against his chest. He set his chin against the top of her head.

"We're safe now," Jon said.

"I know. Thank you for protecting me." Her breath was hot on his neck. He felt beads grow along the surface of his arms.

In his shorts, his staff grew. It pressed uncomfortably against the teeth of his zipper.

Can she feel it?

He angled his hips, hoping to test the waters. He prodded her belly. Rachel's breath grew sharper.

She can feel you.

Can feel all of you.

She wasn't pulling away. Jon's heart was inflamed with hope.

Her hand stroked his belly, then cupped his groin. Feeling her fingers against him almost made him spurt. He was able to hold off by focusing on the top of her head. He planted kisses on her brow, then tipped her chin up so their mouths could find each other.

Their tongues interacted. They kissed hard, clacking their teeth together.

This is perfect. This is what I wanted. Oh man! Hot dog! Jesus!

She stepped away from him. The absence of her was infuriating.

She rolled her shirt over her head and tossed it.

Dumbfounded, Jon stared at her milky breasts. They were small, like teacups, and the nipples were enlarged. Inflated with desire.

She had a tummy and a deep belly button. He wanted to see how far he could push his tongue into it.

Rachel unzipped and shuffled out of her pants. Her panties clung to her cunt, as if they'd been spray-painted on.

She got down on her hands and knees, face down, ass up.

"Take me from behind. That's how I like it."

Jon swallowed, then fell into position.

Enjoying every second, he peeled the undies out of her crack and shifted them aside so he could find her flower. It was just as he'd imagined—velvety, puffy, dripping wet.

He tugged his cock out and poked its head against the frills of her cunt. The warm, liquid sensation almost made him cum. He gritted his teeth together and pushed his hips, filling her gorge with his snake.

He grabbed her haunches and began to hump.

She responded with happy moans.

I'm doing it. I'm doing it with the girl of my dreams.

It might be the end of the world, but this is the best day of my life!

Jon dug his fingers into her fleshy hips, leaving red marks. He battered his rod in and out, enjoying the sloppy sounds and the musky smells that rose from their union.

"Fuck me, Jon! Fuck me!" Rachel whined.

He reached up, tracing the sides of her rib cage, and latched onto her jiggling tits. He pulled on them like they were cow udders. He felt a thread of drool leave his mouth and fall onto the arch of her back.

"Oh, baby!" Jon cried.

Her muscles tightened. Instead of pleasure, Jon felt pain. He barked and tried to pull out of her, but her cunt had cinched up like a workman's fist. Hard, sturdy, and unrelenting.

"What the fuck?" Jon cried.

"You like that?" Rachel asked, laughing in a voice Jon didn't recognize. "Do you like fucking your *satanic whore*, you miserable piece of dog shit?"

"Lemme go!" Jon cried.

She began to crawl away, dragging Jon with her on his knees. The muscles inside her felt like one giant suction pad, adhering viciously to the meat of his prick.

Jon felt tears bloom in his eyes. His teeth sawed together, splitting the tip of his tongue and rusting his drool.

"Stop! Please! Let go!" Jon cried.

He tried to pull back.

White fire filled his vision.

He looked down and saw that the base of his cock was splitting. Blood flowed out and cradled his shrunken balls.

"No!"

He tried to pull out. He was sucked back in, deeper into Rachel's possessed snatch.

She began to moan. Not with orgasmic pleasure, but with animalistic pain. She reminded him of a rabbit caught in a trap, screaming in helpless agony.

Her back broke open. A huge gash appeared down its center, exposing her internal mush and muscle. He saw the knots of her spine, naked and white. Blood spurted from the wound and painted Jon's shocked face.

Rachel continued to cry.

Something lurched like a bubble in a witch's cauldron. It expanded, then burst, flinging gobs of blood and strands of shredded gore.

A large hand rose from the gory ravine in Rachel's back. Three fingered, with talons for nails. Shaded an eerie, pond scum green. Each finger was connected with a thin web.

Rachel began to vomit blood. It flew out of her like water from a busted valve. Even the fog seemed to be stained red.

"No!" Jon shrieked.

The hand lunged toward him. The fingers dove under his skin as easily as a spoon through pudding. With a violent tear, it peeled his face from his skull.

Jon stood and leapt away, not even caring that in doing so, he'd degloved his own penis. The strands of meat hung from Rachel's cunt before the sex organ slurped them up into her hearth.

Screaming, Jon clawed at the red gore hanging from his tattered face. He could feel his fingers scrabbling against the twined musculature and the exposed yellow bony protrusions!

The hand went back into Rachel's body. Then she tipped over and lay dead on the floor.

Jon was fast to join her.

A Spray of Bullets
Men in Fright

"Come and get me, you undead motherfuckers!" Lance shouted before pulling the trigger.

Pagliaro put the pedal to the metal. He spun the wheel and careened around a corner. Above him, Lance wavered, but remained standing. He had decided to take out as many zombies as he could while they were leaving town. In Lance Allbee's head, a dead zombie equaled one living human.

Angus Pagliaro and Lance Allbee were lovers, and they were survivalists. They'd been hoarding weapons and canned food all their lives, never knowing when disaster would strike, but knowing it was imminent.

Had no idea it'd be real zombies. Christ. Life is stranger than fiction.

Lance was holding an automatic machine gun. Whenever he pulled the trigger, the gun seemed to dance in his hands, spitting lead in wide sheets.

The zombies were easily pulverized by the bullets. They jumped in place as dusty globs of undead flesh burst away from their rotting frames. A few heads even exploded in chunky blasts.

Lance got back into the passenger seat, holding on to the top of the Jeep's side door for balance. He was narrow, freckled, and Irish. Lance was a cop—just a beat cop, not a detective. Pagliaro was a working grunt. Black, muscled, and bearded. The two had found each other at the gym, which was where they still spent a lot of their time on their days off, even though they had enough exercise equipment at home to open their own gym!

When the zombies had struck, Pagliaro had used a dumbbell to crush as many skulls as he could, while he and his partner fought their way to their open-top Jeep and prepared to flee.

The streets were in chaos.

Zombies had amassed in such quantities that it didn't matter that they were slow-moving mummies. They overwhelmed their innocent victims before tearing into them with preternatural strength.

Pagliaro had even seen a zombie haul a beefcake's ribs out of his chest with one yank, leaving the guy to flop on the ground like a half-cleaned fish.

We gotta keep our distance, Pagliaro thought. *If they get their hands on us . . . we're dead meat!*

"Watch out!" Lance pointed ahead.

Three corpses had appeared in the middle of the road, stepping out of the fog. The trio looked like they'd recently been killed. There was a man with no face and a pit where his cock should have been, a man with a gash across his neck, and a tall ogre of a dude with organs dangling out of his stomach.

Pagliaro considered swerving, then decided to just hit one head-on.

The car smashed the faceless zombie down like a bowling pin. Pagliaro felt the bumps beneath him.

Serves him right.

Cranking the wheel, Pagliaro found his balance and swept down the road and toward another sharp corner.

Lance stood, resting his butt on the top of his seat, and held his gun up. He pressed the trigger and tore a shambling corpse on the street to bits. Putrefied flesh that looked like wet clay splattered the shop front behind the zombie.

"Fuckin' zombies, man!" Lance snarled.

They saw a bookshop, a place called Morty's. Most of the books had been thrown into the streets and the windows had been broken. A zombified woman with platinum blonde hair stood at the doorway, holding half of a decapitated head and eating the brains from its cupped skull.

Stomping on the gas, Pagliaro sped down the street and away from the horrific sight. Not that there was any reprieve. The whole city was a horror show.

"Help!" a girl shouted.

"Oh Jesus, Angus, it's a kid!"

Pagliaro stepped on the brakes. The Jeep came to a roaring stop.

A young girl rushed out of the street and pounded toward the Jeep. Her face was stained with tears and blood. Her pudgy arms reached ahead of her, and her legs pedaled like she was riding an invisible bike. She was wearing a school outfit—black skirt, white blouse.

She climbed into the back of the Jeep, panting heavily and crying.

"Tanith!" a crooning voice called. "Tanith! Come to Momma!"

Lance stood and rotated, finding the speaker. She was coming up to the car in slow strides, her arms held out for an unrequited hug. She was dead. Her chest had been split open. The pit in her center was filled with squirmy worms. A bat worked its way free from the gorge and flew away, spraying blood as it flapped its leathery wings.

Lance yanked the trigger.

Tanith held her ears and screamed.

Her mother groaned as bullets poked holes through her twisted face.

"Drive! Drive! Drive!" Lance hollered.

Pagliaro punched the gas. The Jeep sped away, leaving the stumbling zombie in its dust.

After the zombie was completely out of sight, Lance addressed the little girl, "You okay, hon?"

"Yes!" Tanith said. "You saved me!"

"Just trying to help, kid. We'll keep you—" Lance stopped.

Tanith looked up at him. Her eyes were glowing yellow. Red froth dropped out of her snarling, toothy mouth. A long, black, lizard tongue leapt from between her chompers and tasted the air.

The girl held up her hands. The fingers had rolled back, exposing hooked talons.

She spoke in a roiling, thunderous, demonic voice, "Thank you for saving my life!"

Lance leveled the gun toward her head and yanked the trigger, as if it was trying to escape from him. Bullets blasted the kid's head to pulpy smithereens, which scattered in the wind behind their speeding Jeep.

Everything had been detonated above her bottom jaw. The lower part of her head squirted grimy fluids. The tongue worked laboriously, sliding in and out of the wet cave that had once been her innocent face.

Lance kicked the chest. He watched as the little girl corpse flew out of the Jeep and collapsed on the road, mindlessly writhing like a speared insect, all of its blood flushing forth.

"What happened?" Pagliaro asked.

Lance shook his head. "I don't know. Something *changed* her, man!"

"Tell me about it when we're outta here, promise?"

"You betcha!"

Just as they turned another corner, they saw a helicopter crash.

The huge vehicle smashed into the middle of the street, throwing shards of twisted metal and rotating blades in multiple directions.

There was a blur of orange as the helicopter broke into blasting flames.

"Shit!" Pagliaro spun the wheel. The Jeep shifted around but was too slow to escape the explosion. Pagliaro felt his eyebrows sizzle and his skin crisp.

Above him, Lance screamed.

Despite the tears in his eyes, Pagliaro looked up just in time to watch a hunk of metal decapitate his boyfriend.

"NO!" Pagliaro screamed.

Lance's head went flying through the air, spinning over and over. Flinging black blood, which seemed to solidify in the heat.

Lance's corpse jumped out of the Jeep and landed in the street, a crumpled pile of tangled limbs pumping scarlet.

Screaming, Pagliaro drove away from the scene. Half of his face stinging, black claw marks ruining the appearance of his Jeep, and his lover lying in the street behind him.

No. That didn't just happen. I'll look over, and Lance will be alive.

He can't be dead.

Not so suddenly.

Not without any last words.

Now Pagliaro was driving back the way he'd come, back into the heart of the city.

All around him, zombies walked.

From Below Where Gods Lurk

Beneath the city, The Young Prince and The Unholy Whore watched the chaos.

They enjoyed the smell of burning blood, sizzling flesh, and the sounds of slow, brutal mastication.

It was as if the city itself was being eaten from the inside out.

BOOK THREE

Gore of the Living Dead

Blackhearted Evil

Coldhearted Hatred

"YOU SAVED OUR LIVES," Lori said, wiping the tears away from her anxious eyes. "I just can't believe it happened. Even after everything Chadwick and I have already seen."

Kern was leaning against his counter. Patsy sat at the table, holding Lori's hand and comforting her. Lori and Chadwick had explained most of what they'd witnessed to Kern and Patsy, and they were happy to be believed. Although now that the dead were infesting the city, was it really that farfetched to consider two people were possessed by evil gods, and that they were the cause of all this strife and turmoil?

They froze before getting to the part of their tale where Chadwick and Lori met up once more on the stairs leading up to her apartment. The recent shock of what had occurred . . . it hadn't worn off.

"I'm just glad you heard us and came over," Lori said.

"I'm glad I have a gun. If I didn't, we'd all be dead."

Patsy nodded. "I'm sorry I ever told you to sell it. I'm glad you didn't, Alex."

Kern grinned slightly, happy to have been proven not only useful . . . but right.

Lori wondered why she hadn't liked her adjacent neighbor. Now that she was in his apartment, protected by him, she felt silly for detecting such bad vibes before.

"Andres may not have been my favorite person on the planet," Kern said, opening his fridge and digging around for a beer. "But seeing him all torn up like that? Christ. Anyone want a drink?"

"I'll take one if yer offering." Chadwick raised a gnarled hand.

"I guess I will too." Lori sighed.

Kern brought them their beers. Patsy was the only one not drinking. She kneaded her hands together furtively and glanced toward the window. The pane of glass was so foggy it looked like a blank canvas.

"You're sure no one can get in through the fire escape?"

"I'm sure," Kern replied to his girlfriend. "It barely opens."

"Well, that's comforting. In case there's a fire, we're toast!"

"I'm not worried about a fire," Kern said.

Chadwick spoke, "You oughta be. I saw it. I saw what's causing all of this. It's Hell. And Hell is *hot*."

"Yeah?" Kern raised a brow.

"It's true. He touched this book and had a vision!" Lori said.

"I believe you," Kern said. "I believe the rest of your story."

Lori nodded. She still felt like arguing, to convince herself that it was all true rather than convince anyone else.

"Let's see this book," Kern said.

Lori handed it to him. Happy to be rid of it while also terrified that it would shatter like pottery in his calloused hands.

Kern stood by his counter again, tenderly leafing through the blasphemous and hardly translated pages of the sacred book.

"I think the only word I recognize in here is 'beget.'"

"Yes. That's about it."

Kern turned to the back pages. "Yes. Here it is. Exactly as described."

He set the book on the table, turning it so Lori could get the best view. She gasped and held a hand up to her mouth. Drawn on the paper was a sketchy figure. A bald woman with mutilated genitals, standing on a pile of corpses, feasting on a severed human arm.

"What is this?" Lori asked.

"It sounds like what happened in the park. What Chadwick saw—er, not *saw*, but—" Kern stumbled.

"What's it look like?"

"A bald woman. Eating corpses," Lori said.

"That's what Whistler told me. He also said, and I'm quoting, 'Her pussy is all fucked-up!' Is that picture accurate?"

"Unfortunately, yes," Lori intoned.

Chadwick released an exasperated sigh. "I hope Whistler is okay. He ran off in a hurry. Hope he got away."

"I hate that he left you there."

"He was self-preserving. I'd've slowed him down," Chadwick said.

"So, you touched this book and you saw a vision?" Kern asked. "What was it like?"

Chadwick shuddered and tied his fingers together. He dipped his cragged head and crumpled his mouth. "It was unspeakable. I saw— Oh, how do I even explain it?"

Lori cut in. "We know, so far, that it's a set of twins that are causing all this—The Foul Twins. They've got long and crazy names, but we know one of them is called The Young Prince."

"The other is The Unholy Whore," Chadwick declared. "They are ancient gods and part of a long lineage that stretches from now to before humanity was even a dream. They are brother and sister, yes, but they are also lovers. And they revel in violence."

"You learned all that just by touching this book?" Kern held the tome and fingered its edges. "Are you psychic?"

"Never been before. Seems the book chose me. Not to help us, but just to taunt me. I ain't seen nuthin' in all my life, up until this book decided to show me Hell."

"Hell? Like in the Bible?" Patsy asked.

"No. Not just a lake of fire with red-skinned devils. No. Hell is much worse. It's an ocean. Only, the water is made of acid. The sky itself is lit ablaze. A big, orange swirling inferno. And I was dragged into the ocean's burning depths, and I was brought to . . . to a cave. In it, the Inninian lived. Formless. Evil. They just fucked and killed and screamed. They have no language. That's why their bible can't be properly translated. It's just garbled screaming and mush mouth. I saw The Foul Twins. They were cancerous growths on the amalgamation that was their family. They popped like pimples, and their juices flowed upward—up and up—and broke through what they call 'The Crust,' the barrier between our world and theirs."

"Oh God," Patsy moaned.

"The first of them to find a host was the brother, The Young Prince. He found a scholar who was obsessing over their sacred text. He filled him, then forced him to write the only complete translation known to man. But if you find it, don't read it! Reading it makes you crazy. The words infect you like a virus. Cause you to do insane and violent things."

"The epidemic of killings?" Patsy asked.

"Caused by readers!" Chadwick pounded his fist on the table. "And every corpse they left behind . . . was added to their army!"

The air felt cold around them.

"He found a host for his sister soon after. Fitting that it would be the body of a prostitute. Now The Young Prince and The Unholy Whore have their army, and they intend on overtaking not only our city . . . but the world itself. Perhaps the universe."

Chadwick seemed to sink into himself. Relaying this information had sapped his strength.

"I don't want the world to end like this, Lori."

She reached out and held his hand, squeezing it despite its sharp and protruding edges. He squeezed back as best he could.

Old Fiends Unhappy Gods

"SHUT UP!" THE YOUNG Prince—formerly known as Tanner Fishman—held his skull in his hands and wept. "I don't care about the order of things! I don't care that I'm breaking your *stupid* rules!"

The Young Prince stomped through the sludge. He kicked a pile of tangled rats and watched them scurry with glee. In a low voice, The Young Prince laughed.

"Rats! All of them! Rats!"

He leaned down, picked up one of the scampering varmints, and held it up into the air above his head. Illuminated by the supernatural glow that radiated from The Young Prince's possessed body, the rat's eyes bugged from its skull. It writhed and wormed around, whipping its tail in curlicues.

"All of them are rats, Father!" The Young Prince declared. "And this is what I'll do with them!"

He put the rat's head in his mouth and chomped down. The animal screeched before its head was removed. Blood hosed from its slick, furry body and painted The Young Prince bright red.

He tossed the rat aside and munched on its head, enjoying the grainy skin, the sticky fur, and the crackling, fragile bones. When he swallowed, he moaned with orgasmic pleasure.

He wobbled and leaned against the nearest wall. He rested his head against a patch of fungal growths and listened to the hum of the catacombs. Distantly, he could hear his father responding to him from the other side of The Crust, wailing with frustration.

The rest of the Inninian family were angry that the siblings had escaped. They were angry that it was the incestuous twins who were fulfilling their prophecies instead of one of their ancient elders.

"You've robbed us of our glory," Annon-Et-Elliph-Inninian screamed. The oldest of the Inninian, he was the father to all demons. In their realm, it was foolish to even look at him crossly. But The Young Prince was no longer shackled by Hell's rules. He was god to the humans, and he made his own rules.

Grinding his teeth together, The Young Prince maneuvered down the tunnel, pulling on his chest with a clawed hand. Human flesh was so uncomfortable. Tight, confining, and vulnerable.

He shucked off his shirt, exposing the pale belly and flat chest of his host.

Soon, he'd have no need of this flesh. It was a good vessel, for what it was worth, but he was close to exposing his true self to the populace of the city.

And then . . .

Sneering, he dug his fingers into his stomach. The skin wheezed open, releasing a sloppy gruel of liquified organs. The gray gore tumbled out of him and showered the green fluids that trickled down the tunnel. His knees locked and his second hand dove in, tearing a hole through his belly like parting curtains.

He reached in, securing his hold on a pulpy, half-melted organ. He believed it was Tanner's liver.

Once upon a time—

He wrenched the organ out. It deflated in his hand, spilling bile down his wrist.

The Young Prince walked ahead, holding the organ ahead of him like an organic lantern. As he walked, the burning glow became a shining light. It seemed to rapidly decay his flesh, peeling it off like a mummy's bandage. Revealing the foul beast beneath.

All around him, he could hear humans—RATS!—dying.

Their screams were sweet music.

Close Calls Unknowing

"You reach your friend yet?" Chadwick asked.

"I called his house. Called the station. Nothing's going through." Lori sighed, setting Kern's phone back in its cradle. "I hope he wasn't headed over when all of this happened."

"I'll bet not. Not since he had a woman to keep safe," Chadwick said.

"Safe," Lori repeated.

Kern was playing with his transistor radio, trying to find a signal. "There has to be an emergency broadcast," he'd said fifteen minutes ago. So far, no dice. Lori could tell he was getting frustrated.

Patsy was doing her part to make sure everyone was as comfy as they could be. She'd brought pillows for Chadwick, so he'd be cozy at the kitchen table. She'd refilled Lori's beer. She also gave Kern plenty of kisses, hugs, and whispers.

Everyone froze when someone screamed from the next apartment.

Of course. Andres had guests.

The screams were crazed, frantic, and battered. They quieted down after a small scuffle. Then, through the wall, everyone could hear *chewing.*

Lori propped a chair under the doorknob.

"Think that'll hold them back?" Patsy asked.

"Probably not," she admitted. "It's better than nothing."

They heard a hard thump and a splash.

"God! I can't take it!" Patsy wept, holding onto her boyfriend. Kern wrapped a muscular arm around her.

Lori sighed, picked up the phone, and spun the dial again. She waited with bated breath, hoping to hear Bowyer's reassuring voice. Straining her thoughts, as if they alone could keep him safe.

I'm going crazy worrying.

What can I do?

There's nothing any of us can do.

Just like the girls in Andres's apartment... all we can do is wait until we die.

The call went to the answering machine once more. She hung up.

A single tear danced down her cheek and leapt from her chin. She held back a shuddering sob and used a napkin to wipe her eyes.

"Where's your bathroom?" she asked their host.

"It's in my bedroom. Feel free."

"Thanks." Lori stood and walked through his sparse apartment.

She was mildly shocked by the scent in his room, then figured that he and his girlfriend had been making love before everything went to shit.

Not a bad way to spend one's day. And they do make a handsome couple.

She looked toward his bed and saw that the sheets were tangled and soaked. Smirking, she found his bathroom door and popped it open.

It smelled pungent. Lori almost gagged. Kern seemed to like strong colognes.

She closed the door behind her and unspooled a length of toilet paper. Sitting on the closed lid, she cried into the tissue.

She thought of Brion Bowyer and his Olga, and she worried that they'd been killed.

Or worse.

Eaten!

She couldn't help it. She imagined Bowyer with his skull cracked open, his brain falling out like purple noodles from an overturned bowl.

Lori didn't know what Olga looked like, but she pictured her regardless. A tangled mess of broken limbs and a battered, bloody face pounded into her skull by the fists of the angry dead.

Get these horrible thoughts out of my head!

She blew her nose, tossed the tissue into the wastebasket, then rolled out another length. She dabbed at her puffy, tear-filled eyes, smudging her vision.

Another handful and the roll was empty.

"Damn," she muttered. "Hope he's got extra."

Wiping her eyes again, she knelt down and opened the doors beneath his sink.

Lori gasped.

Tucked under the pipes was a stack of plastic bags. Not unusual, no . . . but the canister of bear mace was what had captured Lori's attention.

She took the can and held it in her shaking hands.

Lori knew all about the City Park Rapist, known sometimes as Baghead. His methodical practices were well reported at her news station.

Sprays 'em with mace, then wraps a plastic bag over their head. They get trapped in there. Inhaling mace and choking on it.

One girl almost died.

He beats them up too. Beats 'em so bad . . . they look like hamburger meat!

Lori had seen some of the crime scene photos that hadn't made it to air.

His crimes had been atrocious. He left behind a wake of misery.

Baghead.

But it couldn't be! Kern had come over to help them! Had saved her and Chadwick's lives! He was dating a lovely woman too! Sure, she'd gotten bad vibes off of him before . . . but could he really be the ruthless rapist that had been stalking the park?

The location is perfect. We live just a stone's throw away from the park. I've also heard him stomping in and out at late hours.

And those scars. The slash marks across his face. She'd assumed he'd been attacked by an animal or something—

He could just have this mace for home protection! Yes! That was it!

Only, no . . . he had a gun. Why would he need bear spray if he had a gun? He could protect his apartment much easier with a bullet than with—

But what was there to protect? He owned so little. His apartment was more like a prison cell than a home.

She imagined Kern sitting in his living area, hands on knees, eyes intensely glaring. At what? Nothing.

At his future victim.

Coiled like a striking snake, waiting for his "real life" to go to sleep so he could pursue his true interests—the stalking and destroying of girls.

Lori covered her mouth with a trembling hand. Her breath blew back into her face, hot and panicked.

We aren't safe here. We're trapped with a psychopath!

"Lori?" She heard Kern's voice outside the door. "You okay?"

Lori hurried, putting the canister back where she'd found it, hoping it was exactly as he'd left it. She snapped the doors closed, then stood and turned on the faucet.

"Yes! I'll be out in a second. Just needed a cry. Don't worry—"

"Lori. You oughta come out. I have a gun pointed at your friend's head." His voice wasn't emotional at all. What he'd said meant nothing to him.

Lori held her breath. She looked around, searching for something to defend herself with. A pair of scissors. Even a nail file.

But no.

Besides, she didn't want to risk attacking him. Not when his gun was aimed directly at Chadwick. If she struck him, what if he instinctively pulled the trigger?

She thought of every movie she'd watched and book she'd read where she'd become frustrated with a character's inactivity. But real fear froze her.

She didn't dare open the door.

She didn't dare leave it closed.

"Now, Lori!" Kern demanded.

In the Clutches of a Monster

LORI STEPPED OUT.

Patsy and Chadwick were sitting on Kern's bed. Both of them looked frightened.

"Alex, sweetheart," Patsy whimpered.

"Shut up, bitch."

He tossed a length of electrical cord at Lori.

"Tie 'em up. Do anything funny and I'll splatter you." Kern showed his teeth. They were hard tombstones. His tongue snaked out and licked his crusty lips.

Lori nodded compliantly. She threaded the cord through her hands as she made her way to the bed.

"Lori! I'm sorry! He must have snapped! He's never— I mean—"

"I told you to shut your bitch-hole!" Kern snarled.

Lori shared a glance with Patsy. *We'd better do as he says*, she communicated silently.

Grimly, Lori tied Patsy and Chadwick's hands together behind their backs.

Kern swept over, tugged at the cord, and smiled. "Nice and tight. You knew I wouldn't let you slide if you fucked around. Good girl, Lori. You follow orders well. That's a lifesaving attribute."

"W-where do you want me?" Lori asked.

"And willing to serve! I should've come across the hallway and fucked you a long time ago. Problem is, I don't dig dudes."

Lori flinched.

"Lori! He ain't harmed ya, has he?" Chadwick asked.

"No. I-I'm okay."

"He pulled that gun on us the second you left."

"He's the City Park Rapist," Lori said.

Kern smiled with pride.

Chadwick frowned. "You mean, he's Baghead?"

"Shut up!" Kern snarled. "I hate that fucking name. City Park Rapist will do, thank you, Lori."

"But, but he can't be!" Patsy cried. "How do you know?"

"He's got his supplies in the bathroom. He stalks women, sprays them with mace, then brutalizes them," Lori said. "Do I have that right, Alex?"

"You got it. Lori, I want you to sit on yer hands. Right there on the floor."

She followed instructions. Instantly, her fingers tingled. Her elbows shook nervously. Beads of sweat developed on her upper lip.

Fear.

She was learning every definition of the word today.

Kern stooped over, reaching under the bed. Before Lori could even consider standing up and rushing him, he was back up. Kern was holding an opened shoebox. He emptied its contents over the heads of his girlfriend and the blind man he was holding hostage.

Panties rained down on them.

"As you can see, folks, I've amassed quite a collection!"

"What is it? Stop!" Chadwick shook his head, flinging a shredded, frilly pair away from him.

"Here. You ever smell pussy before, Chad? How about *broken* pussy?" Kern laughed as he scooped up a blue pair of child's undies and held them against Chadwick's face.

"Get that away from me, you, you demon!" Chadwick shouted.

"Demon? After what you've seen you think I'm a demon? I should be so honored!" Kern balled up the underwear in his fist, then cracked Chadwick across the face.

There was an instant spray of blood.

Patsy screamed.

"Leave him alone, you pig!" Lori screeched. "He's just an old man!"

Kern turned to her, smiling. He held up his fist, then unfurled it. The underwear, stained with Chadwick's blood, dropped to the ground.

"Crawl over to me, Lori. Hands and knees, now."

Her guts roiled. She wanted nothing more than to take Kern by his ears and slam his head into a sharp corner.

She got on all fours and followed his instructions. Crawling like a dog, she'd never felt more humiliated before in her life.

Lori kept her eyes on him. His gun didn't shake. His hand was as steady as stone.

He pointed the weapon from her to Patsy to Chadwick.

Lori's friend was livid. He writhed on the bed, wriggling his bony shoulders and pulling at the knots around his wrists. Blood poured from his crushed nose and stained his white beard a dark burgundy. He looked as if he'd been splashed with red wine.

Patsy was frozen. A seeping patch of wetness surrounded her bottom.

"Stop," Kern demanded.

Lori froze. The wet, bloody panties (how young had this victim been?) were on the ground below her.

"Suck 'em up."

Lori shook her head.

"You better not tell me no, missy. You wanna be a bitch? I'll treat you like one."

Lori swallowed a lump. "I don't want you to hurt me. Please."

"Please and sorry get you nowhere." Kern's grin was like a scythe. "Now do as I said. Suck 'em up. Or I'll fist them into your back door."

Lori went pale. Dutifully, but with red-faced shame, she leaned down and picked up the undergarment with her mouth.

"I've masturbated into that pair more than any other," Kern growled. "Do you taste my seed mixed with your friend's blood?"

Lori felt fresh tears sting her eyes.

Fuck you, Lori thought.

"Answer me when I talk to you, cunt!" He kicked her.

Yelping like a dog, Lori spoke around the sodden, sticky, salty, tangy, musky panties. "Yes! I can taste it!"

She could. Oh God . . . she could!

"Spit 'em on yer pal!" Kern shouted.

"What?"

"Don't make me repeat myself, whore! I'm the only one talkin' here! I *know* you heard me!" He kicked her again, this time on the side. Lori felt her ribs twang with his kick.

She got up on her knees and waddled over to the bed.

"Lori, it's okay," Chadwick said. His voice was syrupy. "I know you don't mean it."

Lori tried not to bend over with sobs. She drooled out a long, rusty length of spit that zigzagged across Chadwick's shattered face.

"Good. All of it."

When she was done, a mixture of rehydrated sperm, blood, and gunk lay over Chadwick. He blew his lips out so the confection wouldn't go into his mouth.

"I'm sorry," Lori brayed.

"Back on the fucking ground!" Kern grabbed Lori by the hair and tugged her away from the bed. She landed on her rump, barking as she went.

Kern punched her in the face. Once, then twice. Each blow sent her spinning and filled her head with flashing lights.

She lay on the ground, limbs akimbo and eyes blurred. Her lip was bleeding, and her right eye was swollen.

"Alex! Please!" Patsy called from the bed. "You can't do this!"

"Watch me!" Kern grabbed Lori by the throat and hauled her up. She was limp, like a life-sized doll. Her head lolled back, and blood fell from her lips.

Kern shoved the revolver into her gasping mouth.

Lori squirmed and moaned. The gunsight cut the roof of her mouth open. It felt like she'd accidentally inhaled a hornet.

Kern jammed the weapon in, then wrenched it upward. She felt the oily metal shatter her top teeth. Chips of busted bone splintered her cheeks, intermixing with a new wave of warm blood.

Lori screamed.

"Suck it!" Kern sneered. "Suck my gun, bitch!"

She writhed, twisting and turning. His hand closed around her throat, cutting off her air. Even if she wanted to, she wasn't going to suck on anything.

How about you just shoot me and get this over with? Lori thought. *You evil fucking bastard.*

"Let her go!" Patsy mewled. "Please, Alex! Please! Please! Please! Please!"

Kern tore the gun away from Lori and dropped her. Gasping, she hit the floor, expelling blood and tears in one geyser. Her head and stomach felt like they had been lit on fire with gasoline. Lori's skin crawled, as if it were covered in bedbugs.

"You know, Patsy, when you open your mouth at me . . . I can't even *think* straight!"

"Stop! Stop it! Alex! STOP!" Patsy screamed.

Kern fired the gun. The bullet snapped through the air and punched through the vanity mirror by his bed. Shards of shattered glass tinkled as they fell.

Patsy shut her mouth.

Lori got onto her side and curled into a defensive ball. Her head had already been ringing before the gunshot.

Kern stepped toward the bed, smiling wickedly.

"You see these?" He pointed the smoking barrel of his gun at the marks across his face. "You believed my story, didn't you? That it was some mugger who carved me up?"

Patsy nodded her head. "Of course I believed you. Why wouldn't I, Alex? I love you."

"It was a bitch. A bitch just like you. And every time I fucked you, Patsy, I imagined I was raping her."

Patsy began to wail like a child whose birthday cake had been eaten before she'd even gotten a slice.

"You're a monster," Chadwick rasped. "You're a monster, Mr. Kern, and I hope you get yours!"

Kern scoffed. "I doubt I will, Chadwick. Because the world outside this room has gone even crazier than I am. And I think I'm going to *enjoy* the apocalypse."

"Alex! I love you!"

Kern stomped close to her, putting the gun against her temple. She cried out with shock the second the muzzle of the weapon touched her sweat-slicked flesh. Wheezing with panic, Patsy shook her head and began to beg.

"Shut up before I break your head!" Kern roared.

"You leave her be!" Chadwick said. "You leave both those women be! You wanna kill someone? Fine! Kill me, you bastard! I'm old anyway!"

Kern laughed. "While I'm sure God appreciates your selflessness, I could give a rat's ass."

Kern tugged at his zipper, freeing his penis. The organ was as stiff as stone. It seemed to leap out of his pants, pointing toward Patsy in veiny anger.

"You love me, Patsy? Prove it. Suck my cock!"

"No!"

"You did it earlier! What's your hang-up now? You don't know where it's *been*?" He grabbed his shaft and waggled it. "Open your mouth and swallow me up, Patsy. Maybe if you suck me good . . . I'll keep you around!"

"No! Stop!" Patsy hollered.

"Do what I say!" Kern growled. "Do what I say—"

Lori smacked him on the back of his head. She'd balled both hands into hard fists and swung with all her might, driving Kern forward.

Patsy opened her mouth and chomped down just as the tip of his penis entered.

There was instant blood and sudden screaming.

Kern danced away from his girlfriend, dropping his gun so he could hold his bleeding member. The head had been removed, and his tissues were seeping between his fingers. Gray and white, sheened in glossy blood.

Lori stooped over and grabbed Kern's gun.

"You bitch! Fuck! Fuck! Fuck you!" Kern shouted, bashing his back against the wall and sealing his eyes shut.

He unleashed a long howl. Wolfish and demented. His mouth opened so wide Lori could see the fillings in his back teeth.

Patsy spat.

His flimsy cockhead landed on the floor.

Kern began to whimper. He dropped to his knees and locked his eyes on the remains of his favorite body part.

"You killed me. K-killed me."

Lori aimed the gun at his head. "We oughta!"

"Lori! You okay?" Chadwick asked.

"Yes. I snuck up on him while he was distracted. It's okay. You're safe now!"

"Shoot him, Lori! Shoot him!"

Lori thought about it. She gritted her teeth together and tested the trigger. Just a little pressure and the City Park Rapist would be done for.

Good riddance.

She fired.

The gun leapt in her hand.

The bullet skimmed the top of Kern's skull. Scalp flesh and blood spattered the wall behind him. He jerked in place, wheezing and hiccupping, then fell still. A bright red spotlight grew around his head.

Lori cocked the hammer back and fired again. The gun clicked weakly.

She tossed the weapon aside, then ran over to the bed and helped peel away the cord binding Patsy and Chadwick.

"Is he dead?" Patsy asked.

"I think so."

"Good!" She spat at his corpse.

Kern lurched up to his feet.

"Christ!" Lori shouted.

The rapist grabbed Patsy by the wrist and yanked her into a hard embrace. She squealed and struggled against him.

Is he . . . a zombie? Lori thought with mounting panic.

Bastard!

Bastard!

KERN'S ANGER WAS WHITE-HOT.

The bitch shot me!

Took off half my scalp!

If she'd been a better aim, she'd have killed me!

I'll show her.

Make her pay.

Make all these cunts pay!

He wrapped a hand through Patsy's hair and cranked her head back, exposing her soft, flexing, sweat-glazed throat. Patsy wriggled in his arms, and although she'd emasculated him, he felt heat in his balls.

Maybe I can still cum. Even without a cock.

Fuck! But it hurts so goddamn much! Shit!

Chadwick and Lori watched helplessly as Kern dug his hand into Patsy's throat. He squeezed the tube tight, puncturing the soft flesh with his crude nails. He wrenched his hand down, leaving three thick, vertical grooves on the surface of her throat. Red trenches, which quickly filled with blood.

"No!" Patsy brayed.

Lori rushed over. She plunged her own nails into Kern's face, clawing him. Reopening his old wounds.

Shouting, Kern pushed Patsy into Lori. The two fell onto the ground, bumping their heads and then immediately scrambling away from him.

Kern held his bleeding face.

"Bitch!" he barked. "I'll kill you! I'll kill you all!"

And he meant it. He'd yet to actually kill someone, despite his violence. And he didn't think the zombies he'd shot earlier counted! They were already dead. Less than human.

He was going to relish tearing these brats limb from limb.

I'll tie them up, then take 'em apart! One at a time! And who'll stop me? No one! The world is over, and I can play however I want!

He rushed toward them.

We Must Leave But Where Should We Go?

"RUN!" LORI SCREAMED, HAULING Patsy to her feet.

Kern swiped blindly with his fists. Lori felt his knuckles graze the air ahead of her. His eyes were enlarged, his face was coated in blood, and his crotch was sodden with it. His scalp hung open in rags, exposing the white bone beneath.

The trio dashed out of Kern's bedroom, into his living area.

Chadwick stumbled blindly, holding his hands out like one of the zombies. Lori took him by the wrist and pulled him behind her.

Patsy picked up one of the kitchen chairs. "Watch it!" she shouted.

Lori and Chadwick ducked left, leaving Kern open.

The chair shattered upon impact, throwing splintered wood in all directions.

Groaning, Kern stumbled around, then tripped onto his own dining table. The furniture collapsed beneath him, and he spilled onto the floor.

Breathing heavily, Patsy turned toward her new friends and said, "Let's go! We're sitting ducks in this goddamned building!"

"Wait!" Lori hunkered down and picked the ancient book up off the floor. Some of Kern's blood had stained the pages. "I don't think we should leave without this!"

They exited the apartment one at a time, Lori going first, then guiding Chadwick behind her. Patsy brought up the rear.

"We need weapons!" Lori said.

"Do you know anyone else in this building with a gun?" Patsy asked.

"I can't fight!" Chadwick said. "I wish I could, but I just can't."

"You don't have to," Lori said. She laid a reassuring hand on his back to soothe him.

"I didn't know!" Patsy suddenly stated. "I had no idea he was . . . *like that*. He's a little rough around the edges, sure. But I never even considered him capable of—"

"It's not your fault he's a monster!" Chadwick said. "Sweet girl, he kept it hidden from you! No one will blame you."

Patsy rubbed a tear away from her red face. Lori realized that the woman's lips were stained with Kern's cock blood.

Lori herself was feeling her injuries. Undoubtedly concussed, her eyes were swirling. The cut on the roof of her mouth felt inflamed. She could tell that at least one of her ribs was crushed by the kicks and punches.

Chadwick was still bleeding from his broken nose.

We look worse than the ghouls!

They snuck past Andres's apartment. Lori couldn't help but look through the shattered door into the pornographer's home studio.

A naked woman lay on the ground. A green zombie hung over her, chewing on a bulbous organ he'd torn from her belly. The organ seemed to balloon in his hands before bursting, sending internal gruel onto the corpse.

"Be quiet! They'll hear us!" Lori shushed her friends.

Chadwick and Patsy kept their lips sealed as they walked by the apartment.

Lori was almost envious of Chadwick's handicap. She wished she'd never seen half of what she'd witnessed this day. She'd have preferred darkness to—

Bianchi, his mouth obliterated.

Kern, his scalp flayed open.

She hoped, once again, that Brion and Olga were okay.

They're probably dead already.

The trio moved down the hall toward the stairs, stepping around Andres's headless corpse and the deflated body of the fat zombie that had been munching on it.

"I don't know where we could get any weapons. We need guns!" Lori said. "The only thing that seems to stop them is a bullet to the head!"

They walked down the stairs, staying as close to each other as possible. Lori held Chadwick's arm with one hand and clutched the book with the other. The text felt so heavy, she wished she could drop it. But she knew that it was important to keep with her.

"Where should we go? Is there anywhere safe?" Chadwick asked.

"I don't know. I just know we'll be trapped if more zombies show up in this building! And I don't want to risk that bastard waking up and being in an even worse mood!" Patsy said.

At the bottom of the stairs, Lori stared toward the doorway, hoping that she'd open it and they'd find the police—or better yet, the Army—waiting outside.

We're bloody. What if they assume we're zombies and shoot us? Like that poor guy in Night of the Living Dead.

It'd be an easier death than being eaten, Lori decided.

It all reminded her of the strange dream she'd had in the control room. The one where she'd been transported to a different decade, had been a writer, and had battled demons and zombies underneath a small Missourian town.

But that hadn't been an exact premonition! No. Things had been *different* in that dream. It was as if she'd changed channels and gone from one reality to another!

Impossible!

Frowning, she realized that a lot of impossible things had already occurred.

The dead had risen from beneath the city and overtaken it. Two demons were orchestrating the apocalypse. Even the idea that her neighbor had been a notorious rapist had seemed out of the realm of possibility when she woke up this morning! Now, it was happening. All of it, and all at once!

Outside, she could hear gunfire. Screaming. Burning! The city was in chaos, and they were going to willingly walk into the fray.

Were they mad?

Surely.

Time slowed as Lori approached the door, gripped the knob, and thrust it open.

A rancid, fetid odor wafted in and filled the apartment building.

"Cripes!" Chadwick held his nose like he was about to go swimming. "What is that stench?"

"It's death!" Patsy's voice wavered.

Waking in Agony

Kern turned over. His head was filled with fuzzy sparks. Pain rocked his body.

My cock.

Oh God.

It's all chewed up.

I need help. Need a hospital. Need stitches. Maybe they can fix it.

Outside, he heard an explosion. The *fump* of angry flames reminded him that a hospital was well out of the question.

It's probably overrun with those creatures. They're eating their way through patients and doctors alike. Wish I could be there to—ow!—see it.

He crawled toward the wall and leaned his head against it. His face had been clawed open, his penis had been mutilated, and he'd been shot. SHOT! He could feel a rag of scalp flesh dangling off the side of his head.

I'm done for.

I'm dead.

I didn't even get to enjoy all the chaos. I'd only just gotten started! Now that I have the freedom to do what I please, I didn't even get to rape or kill anyone.

God. I just want to die soon.

Kern heard a noise. It sounded like steam hissing from a wobbling pipe. Like gas escaping a stove.

He turned around and looked at his living area. A thick blanket of fog seemed to be rising up from the floorboards. Ankle deep, it crawled across the floor, sweeping toward him in rolling, snowy waves.

Where was it coming from? Maybe the lower floors had caught on fire.

Only, this didn't smell like smoke.

When it touched his nostrils, he felt calmed by its honey-sweet aroma. As if he had fallen out of his agony and into a field of pungent flowers.

He inhaled, taking in the scent.

There was something tangy beneath the perfume. Something spicy and dark. Like rotten roadkill.

He enjoyed this smell too. He didn't have any problem embracing the sick as well as the sweet.

Maybe this is death. Maybe I'm being taken to the afterlife.

He inhaled deeply once again, enjoying the caress of the preternatural fog. Allowing it to soothe and comfort him. It felt as if he was compressed beneath the body of a warm jungle cat. Each breath was firm and purposeful. The heat was organic and throbbing.

And there was something sexual about it.

He felt his cock stand tall.

Looking down, he was surprised to see that his member was repaired. Its head was a gleaming helmet tinted purple. It was as if it hadn't been bitten at all.

That was a dream. No. A nightmare! A bad figment. But you're okay, Kern. Your cock is fine and so is yer scalp.

Yes. His headache was gone. His scalp had grown back over his injured skull.

And the wounds on his face were closing. Sealing themselves up and smoothing out, like clay. Even the scars left over from the woman who'd fought back with her house keys! He could feel every injury and malformation being patted down and re-sculpted. As if God Himself was repairing Kern's broken body.

Wheezing, Kern sat upright. He let his fingers explore his physique. They trembled against his penis. His face winced when a spark of pleasure roared up his shaft and spouted from his slit. Thick, pearly gobs of cum spurted out of him and stained his unzipped pants.

It was the greatest orgasm he'd ever experienced in his short life. It tore hooks through his muscles, spun his stomach like a dreidel, and filled his eyes with hot tears. Shuddering, as if he'd been frozen, he set his hands against his face and cried out in rapture.

"Oh God!"

"No." A sultry voice stunned him. Kern turned his head and was shocked to see two figures standing in his apartment. One was a mutated, nude woman. Her body had become fishlike, with gills, webbed claws, and a mouthful of needly teeth. Still, despite her inhumanity, he was immediately attracted to her. Drawn in by her scaly teats and the cup of green flesh between her legs.

The other was shaped like a man, but only barely. It was a clump of seaweed, festering with sores and cancerous tumors. Its eyes were pimples, and its mouth was dangling open, crawling with white, rice-sized maggots.

"Uh-uhm," Kern groaned. "Oh God!"

He started to cum again. As if the very presence of these beasts was a sex act.

The Foul Twins!

These are the creatures Chadwick described.

The Inninian!

In awe and terror, Kern began to gibber in babyish grunts.

The formless male stepped forward, holding open its arms—each one ended in glinting, golden talons. Two to each hand. Four in total.

"I need a new host, Kern. Accept me, and I'll see that you get your revenge!"

Kern shouldered the wall. He was cumming again. Three times in a row, and he didn't even feel drained. His balls were sore, and his pipe burned.

"Wh-what are you?"

"Gods!" the female said. She sounded as if she was speaking underwater. Her voice was a clump of expulsed bubbles.

The Young Prince approached Kern. His footfalls were moist slaps.

"Accept me, Alexander Kern. Accept me, and together . . . we'll rape the world!"

Kern couldn't help it.

He liked the sound of that.

Smiling, he accepted The Young Prince, Barsipher, as his Unholy Lord and Savior.

Find Shelter
Keep a Weapon

Lori was assaulted with horror.

Stepping out of the building and onto the street, she saw bodies piled around her. Corpses shambled about, chewing on severed limbs or tangled knots of upheaved gore.

They looked curiously at the threesome, but none of the zombies seemed intent on catching them. They were satiating their bloodlust on the bodies of passing pedestrians who'd been unfortunate enough to be outside when the sun was covered and the undead rose.

Across the park, Lori could see fires bursting from the sky-scrapers. One building was tilting over, crumbling from the inside out as a swirling inferno ate it. Another building looked like nothing more than an enlarged torch.

The heat fell from the fires in harsh waves. Lori's nostrils were clogged with smoke and her tongue was burned by floating clouds of ash.

Blinking the tears out of her eyes, she ushered Chadwick along. Patsy followed behind them, turning her head around so often she may as well have been walking backward.

She'd been right.

The entire city smelled of rancid death.

"Careful!" Lori said, guiding Chadwick around a decapitated head lying on the sidewalk, chewing its own tongue and grunting weakly. Blood poured from the spout sticking from its ragged neck. It was bald, stomped, and eyeless. A mashed clump of flesh that could only perform one function, which seemed to be to eat whatever was in its mouth. Even to its own detriment.

"Is it as bad as I think it is?" Chadwick asked.

"Worse," Lori said. She couldn't lie.

"Christ, our Lord! We have to get out of here!"

"I agree," Patsy said. "We aren't safe here!"

"We'll find weapons," Lori said. "That's what we need to do!"

"We should've looked around the apartment for guns," Chadwick said.

Lori shook her head. A halo of smoke hung around her hair. Ahead of them, she saw a car had been overturned in the middle of the road. A child hung from one of the shattered windows, his face shredded, and his left arm removed from his body, lying a few yards away.

There can be no God. None who'd allow this!

Lori's blood curdled. She was angry now. Infuriated.

She hated The Foul Twins. Hated their indifference toward human life. Hated the way they reveled in cruelty. Their depravity! The debasement of the city that Lori had so loved!

She wanted them dead. Even though she wasn't sure that they *could* be killed.

But there had to be a way!

There must be!

Frowning, Lori held Chadwick's arm closer to her and helped him along.

"Thank you, Lori," Chadwick said.

"For what?" she asked.

"For keeping me with ya. I know I'm holdin' you back."

"You're doing no such thing," she replied.

"Hey, he's right!" Patsy said. "He's slowing us down! We can't afford to take care of him if we want to survive!"

Lori glared at Patsy. The other woman looked toward her shoes, already regretting her words.

"We take care of our own. And any other survivors we run across," Lori said.

"I'm sorry," Patsy said.

"Don't apologize to me."

Patsy groaned like a distempered child. She turned toward Chadwick and muttered a brief and unemotive apology. Chadwick accepted it graciously, even though there'd been nothing genuine about it.

I guess we can't rely on Patsy in a pinch. She'd rather save her own skin.

Don't know if I blame her.

Self-preservation is natural, all things considered.

Still, if they handed her a gun, Lori didn't know if she liked the idea of the woman taking the weapon and bolting.

If they found proper firepower.

Maybe they'd have to fight off the undead with hat racks and rolling pins, pulling bludgeoning tools from shattered store-fronts!

Licking her lips, Lori said a silent and resentful prayer, hoping that someone up high would put a stop to this madness before it continued.

The thought that this was worldwide was terrifying. She imagined Antarctica melting in an inferno of brutality. She pictured people being thrown headfirst from the Great Wall of China. She envisioned New York in shambles, swarming with corpses and demons.

Let's hope, as bad as things are, it hasn't left our city!

A zombie groaned ahead of them. Tensing, Lori pulled Chadwick to a stop.

"What is it?" Chadwick asked.

"It's a big one!" Lori cried.

The zombie lumbered down the sidewalk, drooling and frothing. It was an obese man—the size of a sumo wrestler—and he was bald. He held a machete in one hand and a decapitated head in the other. The flesh had been chewed away from the skull. All that remained of the victim's visage was her vibrant, red hair. Even her eyes had been plucked from their sockets.

The zombie swung the machete back and forth, ticking it like the hands of a busted clock. He moaned, allowing more drool to slip from his mouth and dribble down his chins. His sallow eyes met Lori's, and she was stunned by the anger they conveyed. Even though their color was diluted and foggy.

"What do we do?" Patsy brayed. "Do we run?"

"No!" Lori said, gripping the book close to her breast. "We must fight! We'll have to do it anyway today!"

"With what?" Chadwick cried.

The zombie was making its way toward them. It seemed to move in slow motion, and yet it was getting closer and closer . . .

"We need to get the machete out of its hands!" Lori said.

"But *how*?" Patsy screamed.

"I don't know—" Lori started before a gunshot rang out.

The zombie's brow dipped. A nickel-sized hole blew through his head and out the back, throwing clumps of brain matter onto the sidewalk behind him. The zombie stood like a mannequin, then keeled over, smashing its bulk onto the ground.

The severed head rolled toward Lori's feet.

Lori spun around, looking for the gunman. Her face broke into a happy smile when she spotted Brion Bowyer.

He was standing in the back of an open-top Jeep, holding a handgun with a smoking barrel. She smiled the second his eyes fell on Lori.

A woman was standing beside him. Her hair was braided, and she was wearing a turtleneck sweater. Lori assumed this was Olga.

The driver was a stranger. A Black man with hard eyes and thick arms.

"Come on!" the man shouted. "Get in here before you get eaten!"

The trio rushed toward the Jeep.

Don't Go Into the Park!

Rough Riding

Introductions were made.

"This is Pagliaro!" Bowyer said, indicating their driver. "He and his partner were trying to get out of town when—"

"My partner's dead," Pagliaro growled. "I turned back, picked up Brion and Olga near your place. They were fighting a herd of dead fucks. They said they wanted to swing by and check on you guys. I'll be honest, I figured you'd be dead. Glad to be proven wrong!"

"Me too!" Lori said.

"We got plenty of guns in here." Pagliaro jerked the wheel, so they screeched around a corpse laid out in the road. The rear tire popped the head, making everyone jump in their seats.

It was a tight squeeze fitting six people into the Jeep *and* the stockpile of weapons.

Lori combed through the collection and dragged out a handgun.

"You ever shoot one of 'em?"

"Only today. I didn't even kill the bastard," Lori replied.

"It was my boyfriend," Patsy hissed. "My *ex*-boyfriend."

"I hate to say that anyone deserves to be shot, but that fella had it coming!" Chadwick said.

"Well, I'll give you lessons if we get the chance. Otherwise, you can practice on any zombies that get too close to us!" Pagliaro winked at Lori.

"You know what's happening?" Olga asked.

Chadwick was happy to fill them in.

"Foul Twins, huh? Sounds like something outta a comic book!" Pagliaro snickered. "I'd say you were pullin' my chain if I didn't believe you!"

"I can't believe it. I still think I'm eventually going to blink, and I'll be in bed with a fever, and all of this will have been a dream!" Olga said.

"Me too," Lori said. "Me too. I keep hoping for that to happen."

The car knocked a corpse over and flattened it. The zombie groaned weakly as it was churned beneath the Jeep's tires.

“I think I’m gonna be sick!” Patsy said, looking out the window.

“Gotta get used to it, hon!” Pagliaro said. “The world’s full of dead fucks now. You wanna survive? You need a tough stomach!”

“The world?” Lori asked.

“I’m assuming. It can’t just be our city, can it? I mean, if it was, wouldn’t the government want to neutralize it before it gets out?”

“Are you saying that because we haven’t been nuked, that means the rest of the world is going through this shit too?” Bowyer asked, throwing a cautious glance at Lori.

“It’s a theory, bud. Only a theory.”

“Christ!” Patsy shouted. “I’m tired of not knowing what’s happening! I wish we had facts! Not visions or theories. Facts!”

“The ground don’t feel too solid anymore, Patsy,” Chadwick said. “It’s like we’ve entered a nightmare world.”

“That’s what I’ve been thinking this whole time,” Lori said. “That it’s all a dream and pretty soon we’ll just wake up.”

Pagliaro sniffed. “I wish. If this was just a dream, then Lance . . .” he trailed off.

“Maybe the rest of the world is falling apart,” Bowyer said. “So, we oughta drive *away* from it.”

“What do you mean?” Olga asked, holding her boyfriend’s tense arm.

"I mean, we should go out to sea," Bowyer said.

"What?" Chadwick's face fell.

"No. It's a good idea!" Pagliaro said. "We can go to the docks, steal a boat, and get away from all this mess! We'd have a better chance roughin' it out there than fighting all these goddamned zombies!"

"What if the zombies know how to swim?" Patsy asked.

"I'm willing to risk it. It seems better than our current plan," Lori said.

"Which is . . . no plan!" Bowyer said.

"Anybody know how to even run a boat?" Chadwick asked.

"My dad took me sailing when I was a kid. Maybe it's like riding a bicycle. You never forget it," Pagliaro said.

"It's better than nothing!" Olga shouted.

A zombie stepped in front of the Jeep. It was rammed down. Gobs of purple brain spattered the windshield.

"Nuts!" Pagliaro turned on the wipers.

Lori watched the jellied brain matter sweep back and forth, thinning and dissipating but leaving a blotchy stain behind.

"Whatever we do, don't go near the park!" Chadwick said. "Let's not backtrack. Let's go around. I don't want us to run into Mr. Kern again!"

"You think he'll be up and about?" Lori asked.

"We knocked him down, but we didn't kill him. My guess is he's madder than hell and just waiting for a chance to strike!"

"I believe it!" Pagliaro spat. "The City Park Rapist. God! What are the odds?"

Patsy shook her head. "I should've known."

Toward the Crystalline Sea Where Bodies Float

COMING UP TO THE docks, Lori was dismayed to see more fires. One of the boathouses had been lit aflame, and the inferno had built into a swirling, orange pillar.

On one of the rickety piers, a man lay dead. Fish hooks gouged his face and groin. Blood stippled the planks around him.

"Everybody take a gun and keep it on ya! We don't know what's coming for us!" Pagliaro said.

The Jeep lurched to a halt. There was a swirl of motion as the survivors all leapt out and made quick moves to pick up weapons.

Bowyer held a machine gun. Olga took a double-barreled shotgun. Lori kept her handgun and her copy of the old book. Patsy took a pistol.

Pagliaro took out a serious-looking rifle with a bulky stock and long snout. He checked to make sure it was loaded.

"Chadwick, you carry our ammunition," he said.

Happy to be of service, Chadwick began stuffing his pockets with boxes of ammo.

"See any dead fucks?" Pagliaro asked.

"No. Just corpses," Bowyer said, mounting the Jeep's bumper so he could survey their surroundings. "None of them are moving."

"Good!" Pagliaro exclaimed.

Lori didn't enjoy the respite. It felt as if they were building up to another explosive confrontation. Besides, moments of rest just gave her time to focus on the injuries she'd suffered in Kern's apartment. The roof of her mouth was aching, and so were her ribs.

She looked toward the ocean. It seemed flat and oily, as if it had been stained by the darkness that hovered over their city. A few boats were on fire, but a lot seemed untouched. She wondered, if it came down to it, if one of those boats would become their permanent home.

Will we survive at sea? Distilling water through pantyhose filters? Eating only what we can catch, after we've gone through whatever canned goods are left onboard? Is an easy life even possible?

We could find an island. Somewhere untouched by all this madness.

But . . . will this follow us? The darkness? The dead? The Foul Twins?

"I hate leaving the Jeep," Pagliaro said.

"Nothing we can do about it." Bowyer jumped off the back of the vehicle. "Do we have all the weapons we can carry?"

"Yeah. Let's get this show on the road!" Patsy said, holding up her pistol.

They marched toward the first boat they saw. A tall sailboat with besmirched sides. It looked long neglected and abandoned.

"Think we can get it running?" Lori asked.

"Yeah. Should be fine. But we gotta check it out first. I'd hate to go to sea, then find we've got company!" Pagliaro said.

"I'll go first!" Bowyer stepped up to the boat's ladder.

"No! Brion!" Olga shouted.

"She's right. It should be me," Pagliaro said. "You're a good shot, Brion, but I've been doing this longer!"

"Fine. Okay." Bowyer wrapped an arm around his girlfriend. "But I'm following you!"

The two men climbed onto the boat, sweeping their guns around as if they expected hostiles to burst out of thin air.

They vanished into the boat's interior, one at a time.

Outside of the boat, Lori, Patsy, and Olga waited.

Chadwick fidgeted, muttering to himself, "It's gonna be okay. We'll get outta here in no time, won't we? Yeah. We'll be fine. We'll be safe."

"I don't like this," Patsy admitted. "I don't know, Olga. What if we get out there and don't know what to do? Christ. What if we sink? Or hit a storm?"

"It's better than being eaten," Olga said bluntly.

"I agree," Lori offered. "I'd rather drown than be devoured."

Patsy shook her head. "I just don't know."

Confronting the Bitch

PAGLIARO WAS STILL IN mourning. Every time he blinked he saw a hunk of metal decapitating the only man he'd ever loved. Seeing Lance killed like that almost made him want to stick a gun in his own mouth. But he'd been compelled to keep driving. Willed to survive. And he was thankful he had. Otherwise, Olga and Bowyer would've been eaten. Lori and her crew would have been chopped up by that machete-wielding fiend! Perhaps Kern would've caught up to them and done God knows what!

If I had died . . . so would've all these nice people.

He didn't like to sound self-important. Pagliaro was no savior, but it kept him going. Not fighting for his own life but for those around him. He liked to think doing so would have put a smile on Lance's face.

The interior of the boat was musty and dark. It seemed to rock aggressively. Ropes dangled from the ceiling and slithered around the floor. Pagliaro had to watch his feet as well as his surroundings.

"Something is wrong with this place," Bowyer said.

"I know. We oughta leave," Pagliaro said. "Let's find another boat."

He spotted a cot in the corner. The mattress was stained like a multicolored tapestry. Sickly yellows, harsh greens, and dark reds. It made Pagliaro ill just looking at it.

"What's going on here?" Bowyer asked. "It feels like this thing's been abandoned for ages."

"Yeah. Like it's a ghost ship," Pagliaro muttered.

"Let's leave!" Bowyer spun around and started toward the narrow steps.

Pagliaro blinked.

He saw something in the corner. It looked like a shadow at first—

—until it stepped forward!

A naked woman with vibrant red hair.

A soft orange aura surrounded her, like flickering candlelight.

She was see-through. Her flesh was so pale he could actually see the labyrinth of organs just beneath the surface of her belly!

Yelping, Pagliaro held up his rifle and fired. Smoke filled the cabin.

The bullet went right through the demoness and splintered the wall behind her. A small stream of water began to leak into the cabin.

Sneering, the woman showed her teeth. They were needle-sharp and oozing green gel, as if she had just finished munching on fresh seaweed.

She held up her hands. They were webbed and clawed.

Bowyer spun around, lifting up his gun. "Move!" he cried.

Pagliaro juked to the side just as Bowyer sprayed lead. The bullets peppered the spectral woman, then blew apart chunks of the cabin's wall. The stream turned into a gush of acrid seawater.

"Hell! It's a ghost!" Pagliaro shouted over the ruckus.

"It's one of the twins! It must be!" Bowyer held his gun up and glared toward the entity. "What do you want with us, you monster?"

The woman released a cruel laugh. A teakettle shriek that pierced Pagliaro's ears and clenched his muscles.

"Your souls!" the woman brayed. "We want to eat your stupid, pathetic *souls*!"

"Fuck you!" Bowyer lowered the gun and fired again. More chunks of paneling danced off, followed by gusts of seawater.

The ropes began to writhe on the floor around their legs. Entangled, Pagliaro made for the stairs, only to fall on the steps and then be dragged away from them. The ropes hoisted him into the air. Swaying and crying, he grappled with his gun, desperate not to lose it.

Whatever happens, I hope the girls have the good sense to run away and leave us behind!

"Motherfucker!" Bowyer screamed, firing at the encroaching ghoul. His legs were secured to the ground.

The ropes tightened. Pagliaro could hear them rasping through his flesh, digging into the tendons beneath.

"Brion!" A shout came from the top of the stairs.

No! It was Olga! She'd run in after hearing her lover's scream!

"Olga!" Pagliaro felt blood rush to his head. He swung around, the ropes holding his ankles creaking laboriously, and spotted her. Rushing down the stairs!

The demon-woman was approaching Bowyer. Still, he held the trigger down and filled the air ahead of him with lead. The bullets did nothing to the monster. She walked forward, holding out her clawed hands.

"Olga!" Pagliaro spun around, facing the demon, then the distraught woman.

Olga held up her shotgun and fired.

Pagliaro dropped, hitting his head on the floor. He scurried around, struggling to get to his feet. The ropes—still tied around his ankles—were singed where Olga's shot had split them.

The demon whirled, hissing and growling like an angered house cat.

Olga tossed her gun aside, reached behind her, and pulled out a retractable knife. She touched a button and the blade jumped out, gleaming and sturdy.

"You bitch!" the demon spat.

"Olga, run!" Bowyer shouted.

The demon rushed toward the woman. It seized her in its arms, holding her in a grotesque hug.

Pagliaro watched with awe as the creature became solid matter almost the very second she grabbed Olga. The woman squirmed and struggled; her arms pinned to her sides. Gasping for breath, she dropped the knife.

"You impudent child! I am Ill-Et-Ellion-Inninian. Temptress of Stars. Goddess of Lust. The Unholy Whore of the Inninian Family. Devourer of Virgin Meat! You thought you could defeat me? Me? I am death! Death! DEATH!"

Pagliaro grabbed the knife. He leapt up, shouted, and drove the blade into the back of the demon-bitch's neck. Gulping suddenly, the demon released Olga and clawed at the edge of the knife protruding just beneath her chin.

Black ink spilled from the wound, sousing Olga and spattering the demoness's chest. She spun around in a frantic circle, honking and roaring in pain. The knife stuck through her throat cut her words in half.

Brion Bowyer fired again.

Bullets danced up the monster's chest and then punched ragged holes through her skull. She bobbed in place, screaming and crying as green slop spilled out of her body, rushing from her cranium, and coated the wall behind her.

Bowyer continued to fill her with bullets until his gun was empty. The messy remains of Ill-Et-Ellion-Inninian slumped against the wall. Spurting water flowed through the busted hull and filled her cavernous body, then leaked out of the holes Bowyer had put through her.

A long, agonized moan left her, then dissipated into the air like smoke.

"You did it!" Olga wheezed, struggling to catch her breath while she wiped the grime away from her face. "You killed her!"

"C'mon!" Bowyer said after untangling his legs. "Let's get out before we sink!"

From the Fog Come the Undead Masses

Lori cheered with relief when Olga, Bowyer, and Pagliaro all returned from the ship unharmed. After hearing the bullets and the screams, Patsy suggested they bolt. It'd been Lori's insistence that they stay, just to make sure. She was thankful for her patience.

"What happened?" Chadwick shouted up to Olga as she descended the ladder and stumbled back onto the dock.

"One of the twins! She was hiding in the boat! We . . . we killed her!" Olga panted.

"What? They can be killed?" Chadwick was aghast.

"Olga distracted her, then Pagliaro stabbed her, and I—"

"Bowyer filled her full of so much lead she looked like Swiss cheese!" Pagliaro slapped Bowyer on the back.

Bashfully, Bowyer rubbed the back of his skull and shrugged.

"After I wash all this gunk off, I'll kiss you!" Olga said.

"Ah, hell!" Bowyer took his girlfriend in his arms and planted a sloppy smooch on her. They stood together, giggling and happy. Thankful, Lori supposed, not just to be alive but to be victorious!

Hugging the book, her handgun shoved into her waistband, Lori shook her head. "I can't believe it. You think . . . you think we could do the same to her brother? Take him out, and perhaps the shadow will lift? Maybe the world doesn't have to end!"

Patsy shook her head begrudgingly. "We don't know if she's even dead. Maybe they come back!"

"Patsy's right. We oughta continue as if, as if this didn't happen. We can't be overconfident. Confidence will get us killed!" Pagliaro said.

Glumly, Bowyer and Olga nodded.

"Oh Christ! Look!" Lori pointed to the end of the dock and toward the shore. A thick fog had developed, and zombies were stepping out from the fluffy plumes. It looked as if there was a refinery just below the surface of the water, upchucking huge stacks of smog and billowing steam. The air stank. It rolled toward them in solid waves, grinding Lori's nerves and twisting her stomach.

Three zombies were clearly visible. The rest were fog-quilted shadows. Lurching silhouettes with long arms and sharp nails.

"Jesus!" Pagliaro snarled. "We can't catch a break, can we?"

"What should we do?" Patsy cried.

"We need to find a boat and leave!" Chadwick exclaimed. "NOW!"

BOOK FOUR

The Worst Nightmares

Eyes Are Made to Be Gouged

Lori led the charge down the wooden docks. Lugging the book, her gun, and Chadwick along with her. The old man continued to mumble prayers as they went.

"Oh God! They're on the boats!" Bowyer proclaimed.

Lori didn't want to believe him, but his proclamation was true. Standing on the boats were more corpses. They moved slowly, their robes whispering, their petrified hands outstretched. Everywhere she looked, there another zombie stood! It felt as if she'd fallen into a vortex of hungry, chomping mouths and yellowed, fungal flesh.

Bowyer turned and tried to fire at the approaching horde. His gun clicked impotently.

"Damn!" Bowyer roared. "Chadwick, I need ammo!"

The blind man froze and began to rifle through his pockets.

"Never mind!" Bowyer stooped over, dropping the gun.

"What are you doing?" Lori stood still, turning so she could watch her friend.

The rest of the posse was now standing at the edge of the dock, on the precipice. The water looked inky and cold, as if they would fall into it like astronauts into a black hole.

Bowyer knelt down beside an abandoned motorboat. There was gunky water in the boat's middle, and a tackle box had been left behind by its owner.

Grunting, Bowyer lifted the motor up from the boat's rear and grabbled with it. The machinery was heavy, but Lori saw immediately what his plan was.

Gripping the choke, he yanked.

The engine sputtered. The rotating propeller spun, then slowed.

He pulled the cord again. The motor coughed.

Lori held up her handgun and fired into the crowd. There were so many zombies pursuing them it was damn near impossible to miss.

Her bullet smacked into the dry, dusty skull of a walking skeleton. The bones tipped over and scattered. Some plopped into the water and floated.

Lori fired again. This bullet hit a shuffling woman in the nose. Her head tilted back as blood sprayed from the center of her ghoulish face. She slumped against her neighbor, who pushed her away. Quickly, the female zombie was stamped under the horde's feet.

Bowyer snarled. "Come on, you son of a bitch!"

He rocked the cord back and the motor sprang to vicious life. Clouds of smoke left the motor's top while the blades spun. They went so fast they looked like a distant Ferris wheel.

"Get outta the way!" Bowyer barked, hefting up the motor so the blades preceded him.

Lori stepped aside just as Bowyer charged.

He swayed unevenly, struggling to balance his cumbersome weapon. The zombies came toward him, groaning loudly and holding out their hands.

The propeller clipped off a set of fingers, leaving bleeding stumps behind.

"How do you like that, you son of a bitch!" Bowyer roared as he launched the motor forward and scrambled the nearest face. The blades instantly shredded the skin and turned the bones beneath into smoky powder. The zombie grumbled, stepping back then forward, accidentally furthering its own destruction.

Lori fired again. This time, she hit a dwarf zombie standing by the edge of the dock. The creature flopped down, busting its head open against the side of a boat before sinking like a stone.

Bowyer turned the motor to the side, destroying a zombie's head. Gray gel and wormy fragments of decomposed skull flew in all directions.

"Brion!" Olga cheered from the dock's edge.

"Come on, gang!" Pagliaro roared. "You wanna die like sitting ducks, or fight back?"

This roused the group. Suddenly, Olga, Patsy, and Pagliaro had joined the fight, firing their weapons into the rancid crowd.

Heads blew apart like bugs hitting a windshield.

Legs crumbled as they were fired upon, catapulting bodies to the ground to be stomped beneath the feet of their unthinking brethren.

Lori ran out of bullets. "Chadwick! I need you!"

The old man followed the sound of her voice. "I dunno what's what?" he said, holding out his hands.

Balancing the book and the gun in one arm, she went through his pockets until she found what looked like the proper ammunition. Lori filled the cylinder, then returned to the battle.

Bowyer laughed maniacally as he used the motor to plow open a zombie's abdomen. The guts fell out in squelching ropes, staining the decking.

He drew the engine up, carving a path over the creature's sensitive ribs. The bones seemed to explode into dust upon meeting the rotating blades.

Pagliaro fired into the zombie Bowyer had pinned, blowing the back of its head open and sending it sprawling. "Come on,

Brion!" Pagliaro cried. "Don't play with your food! Kill it! Kill every goddamn zombie you see!"

Lori couldn't believe what was happening. The fact that zombies even existed was still foreign to her, and yet here she was—gathered with friends and strangers—fighting back!

One of The Foul Twins is dead. Perhaps we can get the upper hand! Maybe we can defeat the apocalypse!

Her heart felt full and hungry all at once.

The gun jumped in her hands, putting bullets in undead bodies. Blood, gore, dust, rot, and putrefaction spread all around her like a sea of dumpster sludge. Her nose burned. Her scalp itched. Her skin prickled. Her bowels tensed.

"Die!' Lori screamed. "Die! Die! DIE!"

She watched as a zombified child fell helplessly off the dock and splashed into the dark water. She saw a pregnant corpse birth its squealing, undead child onto the decking, not caring that it was dragged behind her by its snow-white umbilical cord. Lori watched with rising bile as a man walked toward them, holding his own innards in his hands, eating the tubes in chomping strides. An act of vicious self-cannibalization!

Kill them, Lori. It's a mercy!

She fired until the gun was empty.

"I need more, Chadwick!" She turned toward her friend.

He rooted through his pockets. "I don't know if I have any left, Lori."

They heard a scream.

Lori looked over and was dismayed to see that Patsy had been wrangled by a herd of zombies. She floundered in their arms as they overpowered her.

"Help!" she screamed, but before anyone could approach, a zombie sank its rotten teeth into her throat. The creature pulled its head back, tearing the flesh wide and allowing blood to leap out of her.

Patsy released a long and low gurgle. Her eyes seemed to soften.

Another zombie lifted her right hand and buried its head in her armpit. It came away munching on red meat, its face stained with spritzing blood.

Pagliaro, who was closest, did what seemed to be the merciful thing.

He fired his rifle, tearing a hole between Patsy's eyes. Both of the orbs seemed to inflate, as if pressurized by the bullet. Her head knocked back, forward, and back again like a jilted rocking horse. Then, she lay still.

This didn't stop the zombies from eating her corpse, but at least Patsy wasn't in pain.

Just as soon as this drama had ended, another began.

Bowyer swung his boat motor into the gut of a zombie, and the blades caught. He jerked around, trying to yank the propeller free and pull the starter cord in unbalanced moves, but his attacks were delayed.

Bowyer froze. He released his grip on the motor and stared, dumbfounded, at an approaching corpse.

It was a child. A young boy whose skin had been ruined with road rash. Lori knew the child instantly. It was the reanimated corpse of Bowyer's long-dead son.

"Bob?" Bowyer asked.

"Daddy!" the blond-haired child smiled, showing nubby teeth.

"Bowyer!" Lori cried. "Bowyer, watch out!"

The zombie child came out of the crowd, holding a gaff hook in his hands. The hook was rusted, aged, and dulled. The zombie was thin, skeletal, and his eyes looked like soured grapes, leaking out of their sockets. The closer to Bowyer he got, the rottener the child appeared.

"Bob!" Bowyer shouted, blinded with insane joy. He dropped to his knees. "Come to me, Bob!"

"Daddy! I have a present for you!"

He swung the hook and drove its curved end into Bowyer's skull from behind. The hard metal pierced his bald head and tore a rent below his left eye, from which red fluids escaped and sprayed.

"NO!" Olga screamed, firing her shotgun at the assailant. The blow took the zombie's head off its shoulders but couldn't have undone the damage it had caused to Bowyer.

Bob fell, leaving the hook lodged in Bowyer's head.

Bowyer keeled forward. He spasmed, the metal hook knocking loudly on the wood. Blood spouted from his broken face in thick ribbons.

"Brion . . . Oh God." Olga dropped her gun and knelt beside her lover, caressing his head. "*Shh*. It's okay. I've got you."

Zombies piled around her.

Lori was thankful that their bodies blocked her view, but she could still *hear* what was happening.

Olga screamed . . . and screamed . . .

And was then silent.

It's almost over. It's just me, Chadwick, and Pagliaro left. No one else.

We'll die like this.

We'll die out here.

There will be no one left to remember.

The planks between Lori and Chadwick tore apart, blasting splinters into Lori's legs and making her backpedal.

Chadwick wavered on his feet, plunging his hands through his pockets, searching in vain for bullets.

Something rose from the water in a splashing rush. It was a blur of flesh and blood that leapt from the depths and landed on the decking.

"No!" Lori screamed, wishing she had a bullet to put through the monster's head.

Smiling, the creature gripped Chadwick by the throat and pulled him into a hungry embrace.

Lori glanced around, hoping Pagliaro would help. Unfortunately, he was preoccupied.

The beast held Chadwick in a slimy grip.

He turned so Lori could see the full picture.

It was Kern. Naked, bloodthirsty, and demonic.

He had somehow been repaired. His scalp was back in place and his sturdy penis was like an organic weapon.

He'd gone through some changes since Lori had last seen him. His mouth was filled with razor-sharp fangs, and his fingers had all gained an extra knuckle. Each digit ended in a curved talon. And his eyes—

—they were glowing bright yellow.

Like liquid gold.

He swept his hand up and covered Chadwick's whining face.

"How nice to see you again, Ms. Lyric!" Kern said, speaking unnaturally. Lori realized that *two* voices emitted from his mouth. His own, and a deep, demonic growl.

"Did you have faith, you crass bitch? Faith that you and your *buddies* could fight your way through this? How . . . delightful!"

He dug two fingers into Chadwick's eyes. The white moons burst, and dark red flooded his sockets. While writhing and screaming, Chadwick's blind eyes were destroyed.

"Leave him alone! Stop!" Lori shouted.

"And why should I?" Kern roared. "Now that I'm possessed, I'm a GOD!"

Lori felt tears ice her cheeks. "Please! Please! He's my friend!"

"Then I'll take even greater pleasure in killing him!"

The fingers drove in deeper, plunging through the depths of Chadwick's cranium. He moaned, sounding almost exactly like one of the undead, then became limp in Kern's muscled arms.

"NO!" Lori dropped her gun and the book. The gun fell into the gorge Kern tore through the dock. It sank quickly. The book fell on the edge, teeter-tottering.

Lori held her head and cried.

Laughing, Kern/Barsipher tore his hand down, ripping Chadwick's face away from his skull with a loud expulsion of blood. His tissue snapped, sputtered, then unwound, leaving behind dark orbital pits, a gaping cave for his nose, and frayed lips, which waggled over his stumpy teeth.

Chadwick cried out in agony.

With his other hand, Kern squeezed the back of Chadwick's skull until his brain leaked between his fingers like dough.

He released his victim, and the blind man's body pitched forward and fell down the hole into the dark, inky, consuming sea.

Lori fell to her knees and stared into the pit. Her mouth hung open and her eyes were red with tears.

Laughing, Kern mirrored her, kneeling on the other side.

"Let's talk, Lori."

Solemn Vows
Unending Promises

LORI BLINKED AWAY A fresh batch of tears. "If you want me dead . . . kill me."

Kern snickered in his duel voices. "Now, why would I do such a thing, Lori?"

"It's all you do. Kill. Torture. Murder."

"That's part of it, yes. But you don't know the end goal. The ultimate plan. Lori, this is so much bigger than just the end of your world. It's the beginning of another!"

Lori shook her head. "I don't care. Kill me. Get it over with."

"Open the book, Lori."

She looked up at the Kern-thing. His hands were draped in Chadwick's blood. His mouth was filled with needles. The hot glow of his eyes reminded her of the infernos that had overtaken much of her city. She saw all of Hell and its horrors in those eyes.

"Why?"

"Because it has all the answers."

She shook her head. "I can't read it."

"You can," Kern assured her. "You just need to look at it . . . with new eyes."

Lori felt something burn inside her head. As if her brain cells were hosting a bonfire. She squirmed uncomfortably, shutting her eyes and clenching her hands into fists. She felt her nails dig into her palms, filling them with blood.

"Just do as I say, Lori. Open the book."

Baring her teeth, she reached out and grabbed the book. It felt heavier, somehow. Heavier than it had been before.

Struggling, she opened it, then she peeled open her eyes. They'd grown gummy with swelling blood. Her vision was tinted red, and through the redness she saw the page she'd opened to. It was as if the blood filling her eyes was a liquid translator. The unintelligible words swirled together and became solid.

As the world ends, a new one will be birthed. One ruled by the Inninian. A paradise of hedonism and sadism. Governed by the Queen and King, and all shall bask in their Unholy Glory, weeping and perishing!

"My sister and I are bringing the prophecy to life, Lori. But she needs a new host. She needs . . . you!"

Lori saw the detailed pictures beside the passages. She saw a group of human bodies flayed open; their guts removed. They'd been filled with what looked like living tumors, decorated with screaming faces and writhing tentacles.

"You could die, Lori . . . or you could rule. With me!"

Lori blinked. Blood fell out of her eyes and stained the pages. She flipped through them, reading as much as she could.

"It drives human minds mad, Lori. Even those who read Tanner's translations went crazy!" Kern chortled. "Already, your sanity is slipping! Just for having *seen* the book!"

Yes. It made sense to her. All this time, she'd been postulating that she'd been stuck in a nightmare, and now the truth was inescapable. She looked through passage after passage, and they all told her the same thing. The exact same thing that Kern/Barsipher was telling her now.

Lori,

you've

gone

mad!

Shuddering, she watched as a picture played itself out. It was of a blind, Black man having his face scraped away from his skull by demonic fingers.

All of this was foretold. But maybe you can figure out how this dream ends.

You could skip to the end and see.

The book flew out of her hands. It flapped like a bat across the expanse before landing in Kern's clawed fingers. Indelicately, he tore through the pages before finding the one he wanted.

"And, without thinking, the last of Lori's friends . . . took his own life as a sacrifice to the Inninian!"

"No!" Lori brayed, turning away from Kern.

In the horde of zombies, Pagliaro was still fighting. His gun had run out of bullets, so he was using its stock to bash in zombie heads. The creatures had him surrounded, but he seemed to be smiling as he fought. Screaming, he swung the gun back and forth, clobbering craniums and bursting skulls.

And then, suddenly, he stopped.

So did the undead.

The world itself seemed to have been put on pause.

Pagliaro dropped his gun.

"No! Don't! Please, let him live!"

"For what purpose?" Kern asked as Pagliaro started to walk toward him, moving as if he'd fallen asleep and was being compelled by a dream. "The next world will be one of great suffering for humanity, and when their race is extinguished, we shall start a new one to torment!"

Pagliaro made it to them. He got down on his knees, imitating Lori, and wrapped his hands around his own throat. Without speaking, he began to squeeze.

"This is a mercy, Lori. He's not made for our world. And neither are you, as you are. Unless you accept my sister into your body. Then, and only then, will you be able to appreciate the splendor of the Inninian!"

Lori shook her head. "I refuse!"

"You aren't the only bitch-whore left on this planet!" Kern spat. "Accept my offer before it's rescinded!"

Lori pulled her head away from Kern and looked at her city. It was burning so bright, it looked like one long flame. The heat was scorching her every breath. The blood began to crisp against her cheeks.

Pain.

Chaos.

Agony.

This is all they want.

All they are capable of creating.

You will be complicit if you accept one into you.

You aren't like Kern.

He loves this.

Loves tormenting innocent people.

You hate it.

You love flowers and sunshine and beauty!

You love the city and its people!

You love Earth and its treasures!

Twisting in place, Lori glared at Kern. He was standing now. He seemed to have grown, and he had already been a giant of a man. He stood a full nine feet, towering above her. His prick pointed like a sword. His hands ended in foot-long talons. His mouth broke open as teeth overlapped teeth!

Lori spoke, "No. I refuse. I refuse you and your bitch sister! Because you may be made of death, Kern, but I'm made of life!"

She stood. "Life!" she cried.

Pagliaro gasped.

He released his throat and began to cough.

Kern glanced at him, surprised by the subterfuge.

"Kill yourself!" the demon cried.

Pagliaro took to his feet, rubbing his throat and growling.

"No! This is *my* dream!" Lori roared. "My dream! My nightmare! And *I control it!* I'm a lucid dreamer, you bastard!"

Kern showed his teeth and displayed his claws. "Child! Insolent child! I offer you the world and you spit in my face? We'll rape you forever and fill your mouth with the blood of—"

"I'm dreaming of the sun!" Lori screamed. "It's breaking through the darkness!"

A shaft of hard light tore through the black clouds, piercing the demonic storm and landing in a spotlight on Lori. She felt the golden rays on her skin, tantalizing and warm.

"I'm dreaming of the dead! They've been returned to their tombs!"

The zombies automatically flickered out of existence, leaving not even a scrap of dried flesh in their wake.

"You cunt! You weeping cunt! We'll tear you apart! We'll wreak havoc upon you! We'll revive your friends and kill them again! And again! And again!"

"I'm dreaming of wind and rain to extinguish the fires you lit!"

Rain fell. The wind blew Lori's hair. More rays of sunlight broke through the clouds but did not stop the torrent of rain. Soon, the fires began to dim, then crawled away. Slithering into the earth and dissipating with crispy, sizzling hisses.

Frantically, Kern began to flip through the pages of his book. He read aloud in an ancient, forgotten tongue.

"Do it, Lori! Kill him!" Pagliaro said. "Kill him!"

"I'm dreaming! And you're nothing! You're nothing!" Lori shouted at Kern.

The monster was shaking.

She realized that the Inninian was trying to escape his body. The flesh began to break in his middle, spitting long strands of blood and choppy flaps of tendon. His navel popped out, looking like a hairy chestnut, then exploded. Blood and pus flew out in gushing streaks.

His penis began to enlarge. Then it suddenly prolapsed, turning inside out like a shirt sleeve.

Kern's screams turned girlish.

The book fell from his hands and hit the ground. The pages were suddenly aflame, swirling red, orange, and pitch-black. The pages burned fast, leaving nothing behind but powdery ash.

Kern continued to scream, widening his toothy mouth so Lori could see down his pink gullet.

"My friends are all here!" Lori proclaimed. "And we're *killing you!*"

Pagliaro stepped beside her. There were sudden claps of thunder, followed by lightning flashes. With each burst, another dead friend came back to life. First Chadwick, then Bowyer, then Olga, then Patsy.

They all stood next to each other, a small line of humanity bravely facing the bleeding tsunami that was Barsipher. That had been Kern.

Gurgling as the skin slipped away from him, the demon was exposed. Formless, gunky, and clotted. Tentacles broke from it and slumped and slashed through the air, shirking back before they could strike Lori. It was as if she had a protective bubble around her.

"Nothing! Nothing!" Lori chanted. "You are *NOTHING*!"

Barsipher burst open like rotten fruit. Fluids sprayed in all directions, tattooing the dock, nearby boats, and even the ocean around them.

They watched as he was turned into a fountain, flinging his fluids and circling around and around . . . being reduced to a tornado of gore.

And then—

And the Next One An Endless Loop

Lori Lyric awoke with a start. Her nightmare had crumbled around her into pitch darkness, and then she'd been expulsed from dreamland and planted back into reality.

For whatever that was worth.

Lori blinked, rubbed the sleep from her eyes, then yawned like a limber cat, stretching her arms over her head and relieving the tension in her muscles.

Sleep was hard to come by, hard to keep, and hard to enjoy. Especially with all the work she had to do.

"You nap?" Brion Bowyer asked from his desk.

"A little." Lori struggled to stand. She adjusted her skirt and checked her buttons. "What's happened?"

"Not much. No one really knows what the fuck is going on. It's like the apocalypse out there. We've got folks on the scene, of course."

"On the scene?"

"Yeah. There was another shooting."

"I thought you said not much had happened?" Lori bolted toward the desk and looked into the row of screens showing the multiple camera angles that surrounded the anchor.

"What'd you dream about?" Bowyer asked.

"Huh?"

"You were dreaming pretty loud."

"Oh, sorry." Lori sat in the chair beside Bowyer. Everyone around them was chattering and dashing about, as if they expected the building to collapse if they didn't keep it standing. "I dreamed about the city."

Blinking wearily, Lori wondered why her eyes hurt. Why she seemed to be seeing red splotches over her vision.

"The city?" Bowyer asked.

"Yeah. It was . . . it was on fire," Lori muttered.

She wondered why it was that her heart was in such agony. Was it the lingering aftereffects of her dream? She hoped so. That could be easy to dismiss.

"The city was on fire," she repeated, "and the dead were walking . . ."

On the screen ahead of her, she watched a man named Bianchi describe an ancient book. For some reason, Lori felt as if she'd read the exact text he was referring to. Felt as if she'd memorized parts of it.

As the world ends, a new one will be birthed. One ruled by the Inninian. A paradise of hedonism and sadism. Governed by the Queen and King, and all shall bask in their Unholy Glory, weeping and perishing!

THE END

Shout out to my $10 Patrons

Thank you for helping me keep my lights on!

Carrie White-Shields

Damaris Quinones

Sabrina Akley

Marc Scharbach (*A Podcast on Elm Street*)

Mary Curran

Don Taylor

Kris Bentley

Pamela Rutherford Cunningham

Carli Love

Shannon Bradner

Ashley Chmielewski

Mandee

Other Books by Judith Sonnet

No One Rides for Free

Hell

Summer Never Ends

Repugnant (The Goddamned Edition)

For the Sake Of

The Clown Hunt

Blood-Suck

Deep Dark

Toxic

I'm Your Papa

EELS!

Beast of Burden

Psych Ward Blues

Low Blasphemy

Scraps: A Horror Anthology

Doomscrolling: And Other Stories

Milton Keynes UK
Ingram Content Group UK Ltd.
UKHW012322290524
443431UK00001B/25